December 2016

Dear Sascha,
Some interesting
from the Panjab

Tony + Sarbdip
x x

Popular Folk Tales of the Punjab

Popular Folk Tales of the Punjab

SHAFI AQEEL

Translated by
Ahmad Bashir

Introduction by
Navid Shahzad

OXFORD
UNIVERSITY PRESS

OXFORD
UNIVERSITY PRESS

Great Clarendon Street, Oxford OX2 6DP

Oxford University Press is a department of the University of Oxford.
It furthers the University's objective of excellence in research, scholarship,
and education by publishing worldwide in

Oxford New York

Auckland Cape Town Dar es Salaam Hong Kong Karachi
Kuala Lumpur Madrid Melbourne Mexico City Nairobi
New Delhi Shanghai Taipei Toronto

with offices in

Argentina Austria Brazil Chile Czech Republic France Greece
Guatemala Hungary Italy Japan Poland Portugal Singapore
South Korea Switzerland Turkey Ukraine Vietnam

Oxford is a registered trade mark of Oxford University Press
in the UK and in certain other countries

First published 2008

ISBN 978-0-19-547579-1

Typeset in Bookman Old Style
Printed in Pakistan by
Mehran Printers, Karachi.
Published by
Ameena Saiyid, Oxford University Press
No. 38, Sector 15, Korangi Industrial Area, PO Box 8214
Karachi-74900, Pakistan.

Contents

	Preface	vii
	Introduction	xiii
1.	Dear as Salt	1
2.	The Fan of Patience	6
3.	Two Thugs	13
4.	Princess Pomegranate	19
5.	The Stepbrother	28
6.	Prince Ruby	36
7.	The Precious Handkerchief	47
8.	The Wise Pigeon	53
9.	Four Friends	61
10.	The Golden-Haired Princess	68
11.	Fate Versus Wisdom	76
12.	The Cat Princess	84
13.	A Bad Bargain	89
14.	The Foolish Crocodile	92
15.	Thc Timid Tiger	95

PREFACE

SOMETHING ABOUT THE STORIES

This book was first published in Urdu in 1963. The Pakistan Writers' Guild was established during the rule of Field Marshal Mohammad Ayub Khan, and *Punjabi Lok Kahanian* was one of the titles in the first set of books published by the Guild Publishing House.

Two of the stories from the Urdu edition have been translated into Japanese by Professor Asada Yutaka, and are part of the anthology, *Folktales of the World*, published in Japan in 1980. Three other stories were translated by a Japanese litterateur, Mr Teratani. UNESCO has published the Urdu edition in seven languages of the world; the well-known journalist and writer (late) Ahmed Bashir rendered it into English.

I had started working on these folk tales about forty years ago. This collection was my first venture in the field. Among my other books on local and international folk tales are collections of Punjabi folk sagas, and Chinese, German, Irani, and Japanese folk tales.

What is a folk tale? What is its definition? What is its status in literature? What is its relationship with society? How far does it reflect real life? In what forms does it present symbols and metaphors? Why are most of its characters mythological? How close are they to reality? And how far have they travelled from the past to reach us? Journeying through different eras and struck by the blasts of changing times, how were they moulded into their present form? Furthermore, what is the reason for the many similarities between the folk tales of different countries?

In the research on folklore conducted in universities and cultural institutions in the West such stories have been carefully categorized, and the popular tale has been classified according to its various forms.

From the very beginning human beings have had a predilection for telling stories. Thousands of years ago when they lived in forests, caves and deep mountain caverns they must have been as captivated by stories as we are today. The roots of story-telling sprouted when man, as yet innocent of civilization and culture, extolled his own bravery, described the hunt, or gave an account of a journey. According to Dr Gian Chand, the art of storytelling is as old as human speech.

If we study the earliest written folk tales it becomes clear that to achieve their present form they must have journeyed many centuries. These stories are the product of diverse minds over many ages. The folk literature of every language and region of the world is the product of the traditions of different ages that has absorbed the emotions and perceptions of innumerable people. Each generation entrusted it to the next as an oral tradition, until it arrived at the stage when it was written down.

A common misconception about folk tales is that they are purposeless, fanciful stories, unrelated to real life. Those who say this overlook the fact that folk tales are the cultural and literary heritage of the advanced and enlightened intellects of today, coming down to them from minds that, thousands of years ago, were still in the earliest stages of intellectual development, and had attained neither depth of perception nor touched the higher pinnacles of thought. They highlight that period of history when science and literature, culture and human civilization were in their initial stages. The man of that age used his limited intelligence, imperfect perceptions and nascent understanding to prepare the ground for a highway over which caravans of science and literature were destined to travel thousands of years into the future.

These stories cannot, therefore, be dismissed as fanciful, unrealistic, or nonsensical. They are the first flush of colour in the earliest history of a people's thought.

However, it is true that these stories give few clues to the history or society of the time in the form that we would expect. They are the collective creation of people who lived in an age when human beings did not have the understanding of history and society that they now possess. It was a time when society was in its earliest stages. People were prisoners to superstition. They misinterpreted facts and were unfamiliar with the character of various forces of nature that are at work in the world. Therefore, to demand patent historical or societal images in folk stories is not realistic.

Yet, one can get a glimpse of history in folk stories. Braves who lifted mountains on their palms, men who kicked the earth and caused water to gush out, those who could tie death to the leg of a bed, and those who could take the sun between their teeth, are all characters from folk stories.

Good and oppressive rajas, princes who pursue beautiful girls, heroes trapped in dangerous forests, fairies from paradise flying in the sky, silver and gold palaces in the control of giants, pools of milk, super giants who carry an object or person from one country to another in the twinkling of an eye, and princesses in distress who are rescued by heroes; all such characters appear in folklore.

Folk stories contain not just improbable, romantic, and fanciful stuff; they tell us about the ideas and literary leanings of ancient people, and also inform us of their views, traditions, customs, rites, style of life, aspirations, desires, and fears. They represent our living world.

Folk stories do have a close link with human life in that they depict some good or bad trait of society, and are not merely all fantasy or farce. It is indisputable that all the genres of literature that we see today—the novel, short story, epic poetry—are in some form or another indebted to folk stories. In fact, narrative literature, globally, has been founded on folk stories.

All critics and scholars seem to be united in the view that *Ramayan*, *Maha Bharat*, Homer's *Iliad* and *Odyssey* reflect some of their features and were all based on the folklore of their time. Moreover, many of the narratives bear a striking resemblance to each other. Similar stories surface in Sanskrit, Greek, Persian, and Arabic folk literatures.

These small differences are what complicate the compiler's job. I had to encounter many difficulties in the course of collecting these folk stories. I listened to stories told by old people from different parts of Punjab but the trouble was, apart from the central idea and the main characters, the same story told by different people had different versions. The same story had taken on a variety of forms and each form was told in a different way. One reason for this was that parts of many other stories were grafted into one story so that a narrative would start as one story and end as another. Distinctive local traditions too were absorbed by the stories as they went from region to region. Therefore, I reassembled the stories, restoring order to their plots, and when I had arranged them in what seemed to be in the best and most harmonious form, I wrote them down. It took me many years to do all of this.

In putting together and writing the stories in this collection I have abided by the following principle: The characters, venues, episodes, background, plots, etc. are taken from the original. However, I have improvised the dialogues, keeping in mind the occasion, the circumstances, and the psychological state of the characters, and have also described scenes. The point of this whole exercise has been to keep the flow of the narrative smooth, in order to make the story as attractive and interesting as possible.

As far as the language is concerned, I have kept it as simple as possible. Similarly, I have rendered the stories in an uncomplicated style. Simplicity of language and narration is appropriate for these stories. Difficult and cumbersome words damage the simplicity and impact of folk tales. The truth, beauty, and simplicity of these stories should not be weighed down with burdensome words. It is after all their truth and humanism that has kept their righteous kings alive in people's heart while numerous magnificent crowned heads lie buried in the pages of history. Even in the advanced modern age of science, when somebody begins a story with 'Once upon a time there was a king...' we are immediately transported to the splendid court of a compassionate and magnanimous monarch which is equally accessible to both rich and poor, and his palace where beautiful princesses live in kindness and harmony with their slave girls.

Shafi Aqeel
Karachi

INTRODUCTION

The first known use of the word 'Punjab' is in the sixteenth century book *Tarikh-e-Sher Shah Suri* which mentions the construction of a fort by 'Sher Khan of Punjab'. The name crops up again in Abul Fazal's *Ain-e-Akbari* (part 1). Geographically, the Punjab is an area that lies to the north-west of the Indian subcontinent. While the Vedic era identifies this region as *Sapt Sindhu* or the land of seven rivers; the Persianized version of the name reduces the seven to five and renames it the *Panj-Aab* meaning the land of five rivers. This is corroborated by the use of the word in Jehangir's *Tuzk-i-Jahangeeri*. Fertile and prosperous, the region served historically as the granary for the teeming multitude of people who inhabited the northern parts of the subcontinent. The political events of 1947 saw the Punjab carved into two regions: East and West; with the former becoming part of India and the latter evolving as the largest of four provinces in the new country of Pakistan.

The word 'folklore' was coined in 1846 by William John Thoms, an English antiquary, and is inclusive of both material, verbal and spiritual culture; all of which pay scant attention to geographical and territorial boundaries. As such, the Punjab boasts a wide diversity of cultural practice which bears the stamp of neither Pakistan nor India; predating it to a primeval beginning which has chosen to treat alteration, adaptation and dissemination with the same generosity of spirit as the Punjabis have displayed towards the many invaders, conquerors and settlers that their history has witnessed.

Enforced by the fact that oral literature predates the written by many millennia, there is an increasing appreciation among academics and researchers that only a small percentage of man's creative genius has depended on literacy. Most preliterate societies have had a vibrant tradition of oral literature which benefited from the received wisdom of the communities they served. From short stories, riddles and proverbs to the epic narratives of the Greek *Odyssey* and the Mesopotamian *Gilgamesh*, oral literature was composed long before stories were written down.

It is an accepted fact that for a long period of time in the history of man's evolution, the only way any knowledge could survive the test of time was to have it memorized. Whether it was song, lullaby, theosophy, saga or history, it was the human tongue with its capacity for rhythmic language and narration that allowed for the conservation and dissemination of knowledge. Speech, in this sense, was the world's first great medium of communication and the ancient world boasted of men and women with such astonishing prowess that they could memorize enormous amounts of material and pass it on from generation to generation. Consequently, a substantial body of oral literature has become the subject of recent research and documentation; interest in which commenced as early as the nineteenth century with the publication of *Household Tales*, a two volume tome compiled by the German philologists Jacob and Wilhelm Grimm. The Danish author Hans Christian Anderson and the Scottish classicist and folklorist Andrew Lang were quick to follow the lead with their own publications. Invaluable as their work was in tracing the similarities between German and other European folktales, these researchers neglected to look beyond their own known world and remained unaware of the vast store of folklore that existed among people of other continents. Though the Grimm brothers postulated theories about a common Indo-European ancestry of folktales, the German scholar Max Muller further complicated things by stating that the growth of mythology paralleled the decline of ancient languages such as Sanskrit. Further interest in the field was aroused by the publication of Sir James Frazer's magnificent *The Golden Bough* (1890) which, despite its twelve volume length, gained immense popularity.

The most important aspect of oral literature is that it belongs to an entire people and therefore, to a distinct culture; it takes many forms of which a considerable segment comprises the generic term—the folktale. This form in turn, is seen to comprise of myths, *Marchen* or fairy tales and legends. Common usage tends to use these terms interchangeably but for the folklorist each represents a different and distinct form of the folktale.

Folktales defy a true definition since these include both oral and written literature. Riddles, proverbs, poetry and the narrative; all formulate the basic pantheon of oral literature and whatever the form; myth, legend or fairytale, the origin and authorship of these lively narratives is more often than not shrouded in antiquity. The common thread remains that of a traditional narrative of a particular people, handed down from generation to generation as it is repeated and recited, suffering additions, embellishments and changes but all the while preserving its ancient core. Simply told, the tales defy formal classification since they combine elements of legend and fairy tale, epic and ballad, folksong and animal tales, myth and fable, all the while espousing universal themes.

The folktale may appear to be simplistically formulaic in that most emphasize the power of love and kindness to effect transformations, just as the virtues of honesty and hard work are lauded or the practice of loyalty and generosity rewarded. A large number of these tales are also informed by a magical pantheism where the animal world takes on the characteristics usually associated with the world of men. Sly foxes, clever crows, talking mynas, astute parrots, wise owls, flying horses live and suffer as men do in the genre of the fable.

The fifteen stories in this volume are neither fairy tales, which are a largely feminine construct usually ending with the 'and they lived happily ever after' line, nor are they fables in the strict sense of the word since the fable chooses to end itself on a more somber moral note. Relying on plot rather than description, these concern themselves with the adventures of largely one-dimensional characters such as the wise old man, the clever son or the patient princess; while borrowing heavily from each form to create fast paced narratives endowed with a rich earthy humour which is a distinctly Punjabi characteristic.

Despite the geographical location of these tales, it is clear even from the most casual reading that essential universal themes are being constantly reiterated. The power of the humble folktale can have no greater advocate than in Tolstoy who adjudicated that the only truths conveyable in literature were the truths that were conveyed by the simple folktale. This is amply illustrated by the first tale in the collection titled 'Dear as Salt' which echoes with more than passing shades of the Lear/Cordelia relationship. The 'love test' at the beginning of the tale is reminiscent of a similar test which sets the Shakespearean tragedy into motion. Though separated by time and distance, both end with the humbling of a once proud king and the reuniting of parent and beloved child. The fact that Shakespeare himself 'borrowed' his plot from a source at least four centuries before his time reiterates the importance of primeval themes wherein the older the story, the greater the power it has to set off reverberations that may be felt centuries later and across continents.

The universality of themes is lent greater credence in tales such as 'The Fan of Patience' in which the Princess' journey to reclaim her beloved (betrayed at the instigation of her sisters) forces her to journey through a Keatsian 'vale of tears' in yet another retelling of the classic Cupid/Psyche tale of lost love. The motif reappears in the tale of 'The Princess Pomegranate' and yet again in 'Prince Ruby' where it is only after much suffering and many travails that the respective couples are united.

Of the many common factors in the tales, the motif of the journey dominates as the thread that ties the tale's incidents together. In its higher form, the journey has long been used as an allegory for spiritual growth, while in its more popular form it represents the sense of adventure which is rewarded with an accumulation of both knowledge and riches. The tales surprisingly exhibit little or no signs of gender biases and are as full of brave princesses as they are of handsome princes—possibly due to the fact that many of these originate from women.

Serious study of the fairy tale form has yielded the curious fact that a large number of them were created by women to protest against their particular circumstances. This serves partially to explain the preponderance of the wicked stepmother/siblings or the absentee father among fairy tales, while escape from these wretched circumstances could only be possible through marriage to a handsome rescuer—preferably a prince.

Secondly, the use of numerology adds another dimension to the tales. It must strike even the most casual reader that the number seven occurs with regular frequency throughout the various narratives. Seven brides are sought for seven brothers, of which the youngest is always the most adventurous and is the parents' beloved child. The prince in the story of the pomegranate princess is taunted six times, there are seven daughters in each of the first two stories while there are four friends who strike out to find their fortune together in the tale of the same title.

The ancients believed in the mystical and esoteric power of numbers far more than we do today. Popular among early mathematicians such as Pythagoras, numerology and numerological patterns lost their power through religious purgings exacted by the Christian church despite beliefs expressed by people such as St. Augustine of Hippo (AD 354–430) who believed that numbers were akin to the universal language offered by the deity to humans as a confirmation of the absolute truth. Numerous patterns of numerology can be traced back to a variety of ancient cultures such as the Indian Vedas, the Hebrew system of the Kabbalah, the Chinese 'Circle of the Dead' and early Christian mysticism. Each number was awarded certain 'qualities' such as 0 meaning everything or absoluteness; similarly the number 7 represented thought and consciouness in some systems while it denoted wisdom according to the scholar Anne-Marie Schimmel, and Christian mysticism attributed spiritual perfection to the number. Striking though it is in its regularity, it would be unwise to comment further on the numerological factor in folktales without a thorough study of relevant texts. It should suffice in this preliminary introduction to draw the reader's attention to the fact and hope that curiosity will lead him or her to further research.

Of the many entertaining tales in the present collection, some read as more Punjabi than the rest since they concentrate on the adventures of commonfolk rather than royalty. 'Two Thugs' is a delightful narrative about the efforts of two men to outwit each other. The blacksmith and the peasant are sons of the soil and their (mis)adventures are the true stuff of a village audience sitting open mouthed and cross legged under the spreading shade of a *neem* tree late in the evening. Each turn of events would have been met with admiration and each counter turn with guffaws of laughter. The end is as satisfactory as it should be, for men can only be friends when they have won each other's respect.

The present collection boasts more than its share of kings and queens, the fantastic and the magical; elements are borrowed from other forms and diffused through the retelling of the tales. Characters such as the gullible bear and the foolish crocodile, the wise pigeon and the timid tiger appear in tales which fall into the category of fables at the end of which a lesson is hopefully learned. Homilies and folk wisdom are at their best in endings such as 'Old people are wise and the wise sometimes exploit simpletons' or ' It is said that since then, no fox drinks at the river for fear of revenge. It is also said that the brute in the water has not learned his lesson, as brutes seldom do.

To those familiar with fairy tales and legend, much of what they read here will be echoed by strands that drift across the individual consciousness much as they do across the collective. The archetypal lost child, the hero, the abandoned beloved, the trickster, the mentor (a Merlin-like figure) are all too familiar and serve only to reiterate the universality of folklore and the folktale. The flying divan is a version of the flying carpet and 'The Precious Handkerchief' builds on the Rip Van Winkle formula. The demons that cry 'man-smell, man-smell' are a retelling of the Jack and the Beanstalk story. Elements apart, some of the tales in the present collection even make use of the classic 'story within a story' technique similar to the one employed by that high priestess of story telling—Scheherzade of the *1001 Arabian Nights* fame. This is particularly visible in the tale of 'Prince Ruby' where the greedy old man thwarts the Princess' desire to learn about her husband's whereabouts each night by begging leave just before the end of each nightly episode.

The only tale that strikes a slightly different note is the one titled 'Fate and Wisdom'. Abstract concepts seldom feature in folktales where characters and plot are explicit to the point of being over simplistic. However, the inclusion is welcome as it exemplifies the great diversity extant within the folktale construct.

In the final analysis, the prime task of the story teller is to tell a story well. If the folktale is as alive at present as when it was first narrated, and is being 'rediscovered' as representative of a valuable oral tradition today, the credit must be shared between the largely anonymous men and women who fabricated the stories in order for generations to be entertained by them, and the painstaking efforts of the collector of such material. The stories in the present edition open up the vast panorama of folktales of the Punjab and I congratulate both the author and OUP for their efforts in bringing these tales to a wider readership.

Prof. Navid Shahzad
Dean, School of Liberal Arts
Beaconhouse National University, Lahore

DEAR AS SALT

Once upon a time there lived a king who had seven daughters. One night he called them all to him and asked them 'Tell me my daughters, how dear am I to you?'

The oldest said, 'You are sweet like sugar to me, my father'.

The second likened him to milk, the third to honey, the fourth to butter, the fifth to jaggery and the sixth to candy. When her turn came, the seventh and youngest of them said, 'You are dear as salt to me, O King, my father'.

This enraged the king. He ordered the grand Vizir to produce in his court without delay the ugliest of all the lepers of the world. The ugliest leper of the world lived near the border of the country. He was brought before the king in no time.

The king gave orders that his youngest daughter be married to the man, since she was so fond of humble things that she compared her glorious father to salt. This was done. The leper could not understand it at all, nor could anybody else in the court. The couple was then ordered to leave the city. They obeyed. The princess was wise and patient and she took to her wifely duties in real earnest.

Next morning she went to beg for food, though she was a princess. People were generous in those days and in a few moments she had enough food for the day, as well as a big basket in which she hoped to carry her leper husband while she went begging.

One day her husband said that it was very troublesome for her to carry him on her head, so she could leave him in the jungle, near a pond while she went begging. The princess agreed and left him near a pond.

The leper sat there under an old banyan tree. Suddenly he noticed that some crows flew down cawing, took a dip in the dirty pond and when they came out of the pond they had turned into silver ducks. The leper thought of taking a dip too. He dragged himself to the pond and with great difficulty, threw himself in the dirty water, keeping just one little finger out of the water and dry. As Allah would have it, lo and behold, he had turned into a handsome, healthy prince, with no trace of the disease on his person! This handsome prince sat down by the pond, waiting for his princess.

At nightfall, the princess returned and saw that the basket in which her sick husband used to rest was empty. Instead, a handsome prince with a broad smile on his face was waiting for her. She suspected that this prince had killed her husband and would now claim her hand. She began to weep and wail in agony.

The handsome prince told her that he was indeed her leper husband but she would not believe him. Then he told her the whole story and for proof showed her his little finger, which still had leprosy. The joy of the princess knew no bounds. Only those who have experienced Allah's profound mercy can imagine her happiness.

The prince told her that his father was a king too, but as luck would have it he contacted leprosy, so his father, the king, ordered him thrown into the forest. The princess replied that since both of them had been rejected by their fathers, they should make a home in the forest and enjoy life there.

Accordingly, they made a small hut in the forest around which they grew beautiful red roses, and in the surrounding trees singing birds made their nests. Now the prince started going to work for a living, while the princess attended to the household. She was wise and patient, and a good homemaker. She advised her prince husband never to return home empty handed. 'You should always bring something with you even if it is worthless and useless,' she told him. The prince did as she said.

One evening he forgot to bring back anything at all. He was approaching his hut when he suddenly thought of it, so he looked around and saw a dead snake. He picked up the snake and carried it home with him. Now a dead snake is a worthless and useless present, so the princess, who was wise and patient, threw it on the roof of her hut.

Now let it be acknowledged that Allah knows best, and the princess had no idea that, exactly at that moment, the queen of a nearby kingdom, having taken a bath, was now drying her hair on the roof of her palace. Her precious gold necklace, worth nine hundred thousand gold pieces, was lying nearby. Its glitter attracted a kite which swooped down upon it and flew off with it before anyone could know. This kite flew into the jungle and per chance came upon the dead snake lying on the roof of the hut in which the wise and patient princess lived. A fair exchange of goods followed. The kite threw down the necklace and picked up the dead snake which was ample food for her youngsters.

Now, when the princess found this precious necklace, she was overjoyed. She told her prince that he did not need to work any more. They spent the night happily planning their future. When the day dawned, the princess took two gold beads from the necklace and gave them to her prince to sell in the market. The prince did as she bid him, and came back rich and laden with presents. From then on it became their daily practice to sell a precious gold bead from the necklace, and in a few days they had collected thousands of gold coins, and everything that money could buy.

The princess, who was wise and patient, built a magnificent palace at the spot where she, along with her leper husband, had been left by the servants of her father, the king. She made seven entrances to the dining room in the palace.

She advised her prince to attend the court of the king, her father, and cultivate his friendship, and the prince did so. One day, when the king was very kindly and pleasantly disposed, the prince invited him to dinner, at his palace. The king accepted his invitation. The princess was overjoyed and started preparing for a suitable feast.

On the appointed day, and according to the programme, the king arrived at the palace of the princess, his daughter, with great pomp and show and in the company of his selected courtiers and ministers. She did not come out to receive him, as is proper for ladies of distinction and honour. The prince alone was at the gate to receive the king and his noblemen.

The dining hall was so elegantly furnished that it surprised even the king. He had never seen such good taste in his own palaces.

After the king and his noblemen had made themselves comfortable, the wise and patient princess, who had dressed up gorgeously for the occasion, brought food for them. She had prepared seven dishes and she brought each dish through a different door, changing her gorgeous dress and make-up each time. It appeared as though seven different women had brought in the food.

The king was intrigued. He whispered to his grand Vizir that his host, the prince, probably had seven wives. But the grand Vizir was not so sure.

When the dinner was all set out, the prince requested the king to start eating. The king ate the first morsel and found that it was sweet. He tried the second and the third dish, and all the others, but found that they were all sweet. It was impossible to go on eating. The king was perplexed. With some hesitation, he asked if he could get something salty. But the princess, who was wise and patient, cut in to say that in her house, salt was taboo, because after all, salt was a humble thing, and when it was mentioned, fathers wedded their daughters to the ugliest lepers of the world.

The king was taken aback. The morsel he was slowly and out of politeness carrying to his mouth fell from his hand. A forgotten event flashed back into his mind. He examined the princess' face closely. But before he could speak, the princess, his daughter, addressed him respectfully thus:

'Your Majesty, I am your daughter, whom you had married to the ugliest leper of the world, as a punishment for likening you, my father, to salt. And yet without salt you cannot take a single meal!'

The king was very sorry for the injustice he had done to his little princess. He took her in his arms, and kissed her forehead with the fondness of a loving father, in all repentance.

The princess, who was wise and patient, told him the rest of her story and presented to him her husband, the handsome prince, who once used to be the ugliest leper of the world, The king was overjoyed. The father of the prince, king of a neighbouring country who had his leper son thrown away in the forest, was a friend of this king. He was informed of the health and glory of his son through reliable messengers, and all were united and lived happily ever after.

* * * * *

The Fan of Patience

In olden times there lived a king who had six daughters, but had not been blessed with a son. It made him unhappy because he feared that once he died there would be nobody left to carry on his name. He went to many holy men of God to ask for their blessing, he was generous to the poor, and to orphans and widows, but all in vain.

As Allah would have it, when the queen became pregnant for the seventh time, the king was afraid. He was afraid that this too would be a daughter, and more daughters were unacceptable to him. So he ordered the queen's nurse that in case this child was also a daughter, she should kill her immediately, otherwise she would be crushed alive in an oil crusher. The nurse bowed her head in obedience, but informed the queen. The queen was distraught with worry. She could not bear the idea of the murder of her baby, girl or boy, but what could she do, poor woman, since she knew how stubborn the king was.

But who can alter the wishes of the Almighty? When the baby was born, it was found to be a girl. She was beautiful. Even the nurse was shaken because she had never seen such a lovely child before. She had no will left to kill it, but the thought of the king's wrath and the punishment of being crushed in an oil crusher that would be meted out to her frightened her so much that she decided to kill the baby. She raised her hand, but, lo and behold, before she could strike her, the baby gave her a lovely smile. And as she smiled, a shower of fresh flowers flew from her lips, and the room was filled with their heavenly fragrance. This was a sight never seen before by any living creature of Allah. The queen, her mother was also wonderstruck. Milk flowed from her breasts and she decided to keep her baby, at whatever cost. She gave valuable presents, gold and silver, to the nurse, who agreed to spare the baby.

The nurse then hastily slaughtered a goat, and soaking some aprons in its blood, went to the king with them, saying, 'The baby girl has been killed, as commanded.' The queen hid the baby girl in underground palace chambers, and entrusted her to the kind care of the same nurse, away from all evil. Nobody heard anything more of the baby princess.

The baby grew fast. When she toddled for the first time, a strange thing happened. When her right foot went forward it yielded a gold brick, and her left foot, a silver brick. Her smile produced flowers. Soon the baby princess grew into a beautiful little girl. Now she started feeling lonely in her underground chambers. On her request, the queen had a palace built above ground with a pretty garden in which birds sang in-between the dancing fountains, while the princess played with her nurse and mother. The gold and silver treasures produced by the princess' walk were stored carefully in a section of the palace.

Now Allah is wise, and it so happened that all the crops failed on account of a terrible drought, resulting in a famine, and people started dying of starvation like dogs in a desert. The king spent all the money in his treasury in buying food for his people from other countries, but it did not help. More and more people were dying. The treasury was empty, and the king became very poor. This added to his suffering and he started brooding. Sitting alone and silent he would often think of killing himself.

One night when he was utterly distraught, the queen went to him and said,

'What is your Majesty's trouble? Can I, your wife, not share it with you, sire?'

'Oh, nothing, just nothing. Leave us alone!' said the king irritably. But she would not leave him alone. She threw herself at the king's feet, wept, begged and prayed, until his heart melted, and he told her of his great poverty.

Now she had all the wealth that the king needed, but was afraid of telling him the truth. She fell on her knees, and said, 'If your Majesty would promise to spare my life, your troubles will all vanish.'

The king was astonished at this. He hardly believed her when he agreed not to punish her. The queen told him the story of his seventh daughter whose laughter produced flowers, and whose feet brought forth bricks of gold and silver, which she had saved for bad times such as these. The king was overjoyed and went to see his beautiful daughter whose laughter produced flowers, and feet yielded bricks of gold and silver. The queen gave him the numerous gold and silver bricks that she had saved, and with them he bought enough food for his subjects.

Prosperity came back to the kingdom and the king became extremely fond of his youngest child. This made her six older sisters very jealous of her.

After some time the king was invited by another king who ruled over a neighbouring country. Before he set out on the journey, he sent seven slave girls to his seven daughters to find out what presents they would like to have on his return. The six conveyed their wishes, but the seventh, the princess whose laughter produced flowers, and feet bricks of gold and silver, was saying her prayers when the slave girl entered with the king's message. Now you cannot speak when saying your prayers, so, the princess said to the slave girl, 'Have patience,' and continued her prayers. The girl went back to the king and said, 'Your Majesty, the princess wants patience.'

The king noted it in his diary, and left the town, travelling in great splendour and luxury to the neighbouring kingdom. On his return he brought, and delivered, to his six daughters, the presents they had asked for and to the seventh, he gave a small box saying, 'Princess, this is the 'patience' that you wanted for a gift.'

The princess was dismayed. Her six older sisters had rich and costly novelties, but her father had brought her only a small, plain box. She did not understand. Saying nothing, she went to her chamber, and put the box down carelessly in a corner.

The night was hot and humid and there was no breeze from the garden. The candle burned dimly, shedding a pale light in the room. The princess was perspiring. She needed a fan to blow some breeze on her rosy cheeks which were wet with sweat. But there was no fan in the room. She looked around and saw the ugly box which her father had brought her for a present. Hoping to use its lid for a fan, she opened it for the first time, and guess what it contained? A most wonderful fan, lighter than air, and costlier than gold, was lying in the ugly box. She took it out at once, but before it could blow a cool breeze over her burning face, a most handsome prince stood before her, with eyes full of love. The princess was taken aback at the spectacle of his manly beauty, then she fainted. The prince sprinkled rose water on her face and when she came to, he told her that he was the prince of the fan of patience, and that he was at her service, so she had nothing to fear. He held her delicate hand and soon they were talking like two children. The prince told her that whenever she wanted him to come, she only had to touch the fan.

Then this became the daily practice of the princess. She would call him as soon as night fell, talk to him the whole night, and send him away before morning. Soon they fell in love.

The princess met her beloved secretly, but as they say, perfume and love cannot be hidden for long. At first, the sneaky slave girls, then the six jealous sisters, came to know of their affair. They decided to stop it. They became very friendly with the princess, who was young and inexperienced in these matters. She took their show of affection for real and began to trust them. They wanted to see the prince of the fan, her love, and she was only too glad to oblige. On the appointed evening, all the six came to her chambers, and offered to make the prince's bed themselves instead of allowing the slave girls to do it. The princess willingly agreed. Now they made the bed, all six of them, but underneath the sheet, they spread pieces of broken glass, with edges sharper than a knife. After this they asked their sister that the prince be called. She, poor innocent, happily took the fan out of the ugly box and in the twinkling of an eye, the beautiful prince was there. He was a rare sight to see. The six of them felt even more jealous of their sister, and after polite, empty words, withdrew, suggesting that it was late in the night, and time for the prince to rest, whose bed they had made.

The prince fell on the bed and the pieces of broken glass, with edges sharper than a knife, cut into his body. As soon as he began to bleed, the prince disappeared. The princess was perplexed. She took the fan out again and again, but the prince would not come. Not only that: now her laughter produced no flowers, and her feet no bricks of gold and silver. She lost her charm, and with a broken heart, she set out alone to find the prince of her dreams. She knew that her sisters had cheated her.

Disguised as a man, she went into the forest in search of her prince, but without any success. She lived on water from the springs, and berries of the forest. Her feet bleeding and her body tired, she walked on, until one day, she fell on the ground, exhausted and broken. She could not get up.

On a tree nearby, sat a parrot and a myna bird, watching her. The myna had a golden heart and was very sorry for what she saw. She looked at the parrot who was laughing. It made the myna very angry, but the parrot said, 'Do not be angry with me. I am not laughing at her plight!' 'Then why are you laughing?' demanded the myna. The parrot became serious, and said, 'I was laughing because it struck me how little human beings know about themselves, and how much they suffer for how little! Now look at this princess. She is looking for her prince, who lives a few miles to the west. If she takes that course, she will find him. He has strange wounds which they do not know how to treat. But if she takes our dropping and uses it for ointment he will recover immediately. But as I said, how little do these poor human beings know!'

The princess, though only half conscious, listened to them carefully. Stirred by a new courage the blood rushed in her veins. She got up, and first she collected the droppings of the parrot and the myna. Then she set out west and walked tirelessly and bravely until she reached a city, outside whose gates there was a big drum.

She was still in a man's dress. The keeper of the drum told her that their prince had strange wounds which nobody had been able to cure, and the king, his father was now much disgusted with the physicians. He had declared that he would give half his kingdom to anybody who would treat the prince's wounds. But if he failed, he would be beheaded. The drum had been placed by the city gates for those who dared to take up the challenge. This was the greatest moment in the princess's life. She beat the drum louder than anybody had done before, and was immediately taken to the king. She was willing to try to cure the prince, and face death if she failed. She was shown into the prince's bedchamber at once. She saw him, but controlled her feelings. Her strange ointment was ready. She applied it gently to each wound. The prince immediately felt better, but he did not have the faintest idea who his physician was.

In a few more days his wounds had healed and the lustre of his skin was back. Once more he was radiantly handsome. The prince was overjoyed.

There was great rejoicing the day the prince was proclaimed completely recovered. He put on his regal dress and came to the court to meet his father the king, who was attended by all his splendidly attired noblemen. But the poor physician waiting outside was in the same shabby garments in which he had arrived, and would not change them for the occasion, though many beseeched him to do so.

While the king was sitting on his throne, with the prince to his right and the noble courtiers in their respective seats, the physician was announced. He entered and stood, silently. At this the king rose to thank the physician for his great deed. He offered him not only the promised half of his kingdom but also whatever he desired in addition to it. The physician had only to say the word, and he would get what he wanted.

All the court waited eagerly, but the physician stood silently, looking at the prince.

'Nothing, Your Majesty' said the physician, 'I need nothing. Whatever God and you have given me already is enough for me' 'No, no. We urge you to ask for something, physician, whatever you like.' insisted the king. 'Nothing my Lord. God and you have given me enough.' 'Speak sir, we ask you for the third time' roared the king. At this the physician looked straight into the king's eyes, and said, 'If Your Majesty really wants to reward me, and I have Your Majesty's word that I will be given what I ask for, then I ask you for the prince himself. No less, no more.'

At this strange demand there was pin drop silence in the court. Meanwhile from the 'physician's' tattered garments stepped out the dazzling figure of the princess. Her prince recognised her at once, and overjoyed to see her, he stood up. She smiled. As she smiled, flowers fell from her rosy lips and she walked towards her prince. As she walked her right foot yielded a brick of gold and her left, a brick of silver, right there for everybody to see and pick up.

* * * * *

Two Thugs

Not very long ago, there lived a peasant who was well known in the neighbouring villages for his thuggery. He could change garbs and wear a new face in no time, and without much equipment. Other thugs of the area paid him homage.

One day the peasant set out on an expedition, with a pitcher full of *ghee*[1] on his head. On the way he met a blacksmith, another accomplished thug, who was now looking around for work. He carried with him a sword, which was made of silver. The two were eager to match their wits, and agreed to exchange their goods. The peasant took the silver sword and gave his pitcher of ghee to the blacksmith. They parted ways happily. The peasant turned back and reached home before dusk. He told his wife that he had met a gullible fellow who was only too glad to exchange his silver sword with his pitcher of ghee which actually contained not ghee but water. He was gloating at his own cleverness, while his wife examined the sword. Suddenly she started wailing and beating her breast. 'What is the matter with you, woman?' asked the peasant, in surprise.

'You have been ruined, you have been ruined!' cried his wife.

'Come, come, how can I be ruined?'

'Well, this sword is not made of silver,' said the woman angrily. 'It is made of ordinary wood, over which the man has cleverly wrapped some silver foil. Look, you fool.'

And the peasant looked at the naked wood, and was full of shame and anger at having been cheated by a nobody.

Meanwhile, the blacksmith reached home equally joyfully, thinking he had cheated the peasant, and was now equally frustrated. He could not look straight into the eyes of his wife who made fun of him, something no man of honour can bear. He decided to even up with the peasant, and immediately left for his village.

The peasant welcomed the man to his home. They were polite to each other. They talked of the weather, of the crops, of the falling morals of the younger generation, and of other similar problems, which actually hurt none of them, and for which they could not care less. Neither of them said a word about their recent exchange of goods, even though both of them felt cheated. As night fell, the peasant's wife served a sumptuous dinner to the two friends who enjoyed every morsel of it. As they finished, water was brought in a gold container for them to wash their hands, and the inevitable *hookah*[2] was prepared, and ready to be smoked in peace. The blacksmith decided to steal the gold water container and prove to the peasant that he was the more cunning of the two, and had nimbler fingers. But the peasant was no novice. He understood his guest, though he continued to feign innocence.

As bedtime approached, beds were made, and the two lay down to rest. The blacksmith noted that the gold container was hung from the ceiling, right above the peasant's bed. He closed his eyes so that his host should go to sleep. He planned to keep awake until the peasant went to sleep, then he would bolt with the gold container and thus take his revenge.

Soon, the peasant started snoring. The blacksmith got up softly as a cat, but when he tried to remove the container, he found it filled with water, which would spill on the face of the sleeping peasant, if anybody touched it, causing him to wake up. The blacksmith thought for a while. He was not prepared to be outwitted. He looked at the cold ashes in the hookah bowl and an idea came to him. He poured all the ashes, slowly, into the container. The ashes absorbed the water, which would not now spill. He then removed the gold container from its hanger, went out, and digging a hole under a banyan tree outside, buried it. He came back, and went to sleep.

The peasant woke early and found the container gone. He got up and looked around. Fresh footprints led him to the place where the container was buried. He dug it out, and went back to sleep.

Both of them were awakened by the peasant's wife, who had brought fresh milk for breakfast in the same gold container. The blacksmith was beaten again.

Now both of them acknowledged their great art and became friends. They decided to join hands and go out on an expedition together, firmly believing that men of such great talent as they were could never be outwitted, especially if they pooled their expertise.

They travelled for many days, until they reached the outskirts of a city, where they found a great crowd of people grieving over a coffin. They made enquiries and were told that a great landlord, a nobleman, had died, one who had been generous, honest, and just.

The two hatched a plan. The blacksmith went to the graveyard. The peasant went to the crowd, and started wailing loudly. The crowd of mourners was inattentive to his mourning. There was none who knew him.

When the coffin was lifted he followed it weeping. The sons of the great nobleman were perplexed. They wanted to know who he was that was crying his heart out for their father, though they did not know him at all.

He told them that he was a trader friend of their noble father, who used to bring him novelties from far and near. For fear of highwaymen, he sometimes used to keep his money with their father as trust. The previous year when he went north, he had left ten thousand silver pieces with him. He returned today to find that his dear friend had passed away. 'I have lost my friend as well as my money. Oh! cursed be me.' And he started wailing again.

The sons of the nobleman were puzzled. 'But how can you prove that our noble father owed you ten thousand silver coins?' They asked.

'God is my only witness,' said the cunning peasant. 'But if you insist, we shall ask the grave.' They looked at each other. Then the eldest son spoke, 'I've never heard of such a thing!' 'Seeing is believing' said the peasant. 'Your father was a holy man. His spirit will speak.'

The brothers went with the peasant to the grave, in which they had laid the dead body. They said prayers for the soul of the dear departed, and then turned to the peasant.

'Now let us have your proof. Let the grave speak.'

The peasant went round the grave seven times. After the last round, he stood solemnly for a moment, then muttered a prayer, while everybody watched and waited. Suddenly a voice came from the grave.

'I owe him ten thousand silver pieces. Unless this debt is paid, my soul cannot be at rest, hark ye my sons.' The sons and the rest of the people heard it. Doubtless they had to pay, on behalf of their father, ten thousand silver pieces to his friend the peasant. The dead man had spoken. But of course it was not the dead man who had spoken, for the dead never speak; it was the peasant's friend, the blacksmith, who had dug a tunnel to the grave, and was now hidden in it. He was speaking for the dead man. The sons of the nobleman immediately paid off their father's debt.

On receiving ten thousand silver coins, the peasant's greed grew even greater. While his blacksmith friend was still hiding in the grave, he loaded his money bags on a donkey, and went back to his village. He was after all the greater of the two thugs.

The blacksmith waited for some time for the peasant to come to him. Then he understood. He bought a good horse and a pair of valuable female footwear, and rode as fast as he could towards the village of the peasant. In a few hours he caught up with the peasant on his slow moving donkey, but instead of accosting him, took a detour, and went ahead of the peasant. Then he dropped one shoe from the pair of costly female footwear, rode on ahead for some distance on the same road, dropped the second shoe, and hid himself in a cluster of trees to watch.

The peasant saw one piece of valuable female footwear lying on the ground, stopped, and took a good look at it. But alas! It was only one of a pair—a useless thing. He threw it away and went on. Soon he came upon the second shoe. He stopped again, and thought that the pair, would make a fine gift for his wife. So he decided to go back and bring the other shoe too. The donkey was tired, and no one was around, so he let the donkey rest and graze, while he went back for the shoe on foot.

The blacksmith came out of hiding, took the silver from the donkey's back, and rode off with it, now its sole master.

He reached his home and buried the whole treasure in the little courtyard of his house. Then he instructed his wife thus:

'When the peasant comes to ask for me, start wailing and weeping. Tell him that I had gone with him, and since I have not returned it means that surely he has murdered me. This will upset him, and he will go away for fear of the *Qazi*.[3] Then we will live a happy life. Meanwhile, I will be in hiding under the old bridge. You must bring me meals everyday till there is no chance of his coming back.' After giving her these instructions he left for the bridge.

The peasant returned with the footwear to find his money gone. There were the fresh footprints of a horse, and he recognized the footprints of the blacksmith, nearby. He realized that his friend had outwitted him and rushed to his house.

One look at his face and the blacksmith's wife put up a grand show of crying and wailing as instructed by her husband. She accused him of murdering her husband and making her a widow, with no means of subsistence. The peasant did not believe her, but what could he do?

He was crossing the bridge under which his friend was hiding. Per chance, the blacksmith coughed, and the peasant heard him and knew he was there. Straightaway he made a plan and returned to the neighbourhood of the blacksmith, where an old hag lived in poverty. The peasant gave her some money, and asked her to borrow a dress for an hour from the blacksmith's wife. The old hag was an expert in these matters, and in a few moments, she came back with the dress, which she had promised to return in an hour.

The peasant put on the dress, and with a cup of rotten lintels which had begun to stink, and a couple of loaves of burnt bread, he went to the bridge, where his friend was hiding. He was hungry, and it was dark, so he could not see the peasant's face. He took him to be his wife and started eating. But the food was not fit to eat even for a dog. He was furious.

'Now what the devil do you mean by bringing this rotten stuff for me to eat. Do I not earn money for you?' He said.

The peasant feigned the women's voice and moaned, 'There is no money at home. None at all.' The blacksmith kicked him in the back and said, 'You are a strange woman. The money, buried in the courtyard is not your father's. It is mine. Go dig it out and spend a part of it on my food.

The peasant ran back to the old hag and returned the dress. The old hag returned it to the blacksmith's wife as promised. She was getting late for her husband's meal. She left immediately with a large carrier now, full of food.

As soon as she left, the peasant entered her house, and in a short while dug out all the hidden wealth.

In the meantime, when the blacksmith's wife reached her husband with food, he was surprised. He thought for a while and understood. He ran back to his house, only to find every penny gone. He rode to the village of his friend.

The peasant welcomed him home, and niceties were exchanged. Then they agreed that both of them were men of high talent, none better or worse than the other. They became good friends. Thereafter they divided their loot equally. The peasant gave the old gold container to the blacksmith as a token of his friendship.

* * * * *

NOTES

1. *Ghee*: Cooking oil prepared by boiling fresh butter for cleaning preservation.
2. *Hookah*: A waterpipe Hubble Bubble.
3. *Qazi*: A judicial officer.

Princess Pomegranate

Once upon a time there ruled over a certain kingdom a virtuous king who was a father of seven sons. In the olden days it was customary for royal houses to settle the marriages of their children through emissaries. So when all his sons grew up into handsome youths, the king thought of seeking brides for them from a royal house of equal virtue and magnificence as his. So he sent his royal emissary in search of such a house, which was moreover, blessed with seven daughters.

The emissary set out on his mission. He wandered from one kingdom to another, through desert and plain, but all his efforts were in vain.

One night, while he was resting in a wayside inn, his heart was heavy. He was feeling lonely and dispirited, and in order to lighten his mood he decided to talk to the traveller in the next room, an elderly man, wise, grand in manner, and with a beard one could trust.

On hearing his story, the wise traveller's eyes lit up with joy. 'I have the same mission,' he said, 'My king has seven daughters, and I am his emissary, in search of a house of equal virtue and magnificence, blessed with seven sons, for their happy union. My troubles are now over.'

Then the two happy men started talking about the glories of the two houses, their fortunes and triumphs, and peace and prosperity in the two kingdoms. The matches were made as the stars quit the skies, and a new day dawned. Then the two returned to their respective kingdoms, their missions completed.

After rewarding his emissary handsomely, the king with seven sons called his children and gave them the happy news. The princes were obedient sons. May the Lord bless everybody with obedient sons. They bowed their heads in acceptance of their father's will, and the king left his chamber to instruct his grand vizir to make the necessary arrangements.

The arrangements were soon made. On the appointed day, when the procession was to start, the six older sons came riding on their ferocious steeds, but the seventh, the youngest, did not come. The king called him. He came and bowed, and prayed that he did not want to be married yet. He had no special argument, though. Now everybody knows, that the youngest son is always the dearest. The king did not want to force him. He therefore rode with his six sons, leaving the youngest behind.

The marriage party returned with six princesses, leaving the youngest princess, the seventh sister, unmarried in their father's royal house. The six brothers and their wives consulted together and decided to persuade the young man to marry. The mission was assigned to the brides who were tender with the joy of marriage and concerned for their sister.

They called the prince to a feast, and entertained him with superb dance and music, which the boy relished. Finding him happy and relaxed, the eldest of the six, cleverly and wisely, started a pleasant conversation with him, in which she suggested that he should now be married. The mention of his marriage changed the prince's mood. He became stiff and cold and plainly stated that he was not prepared to be married yet. His sister-in-law, tried to argue, but finding him adamant, taunted him by saying, that if he was not prepared to wed their sister, he was perhaps thinking of marrying Princess Pomegranate.

One by one, the rest of the sisters-in-law too invited the prince. Each of them entertained him, flattered him, and in the end tried to persuade him to marry their sister. His response was always the same; that he did not wish to marry yet. Each time his answer drew the same taunt from every sister-in-law, that perhaps it was Princess Pomegranate the prince was thinking of marrying.

The prince heard this taunt six times, and each time left the party, without uttering a single word. The taunt stuck in his mind and he could not sleep. Then one night, under the starry sky, he decided to marry Princess Pomegranate, or no one else, as his answer to the taunt.

He woke up weary in the morning, dressed, and went to the king his father. He told him the whole story, and sought his permission to leave, in search of Princess Pomegranate, who alone he would wed.

The king was a kind and wise father, and knew that in this wild chase, his son would lose his life, like many other princes of far and near, who had set out on this very search. So far nobody had ever been able to find Princess Pomegranate. He tried his best to dissuade his son. He even wept. But youth has no ears to hear, when the heart leads the way. The prince was determined. The king was helpless.

Then the prince went to his mother to bid her farewell. She too tried to dissuade him but he did not listen to her appeals. He said goodbye to his brothers and sisters-in-law, and announced that he would either come back with Princess Pomegranate, or perish.

He set out towards the east. After a long and lonely journey, he came upon a desolate garden. He was thirsty. He decided to drink some water, and rest for a while. It was a garden of pomegranate trees. To his utter surprise, he found that there was no one in the garden, and except for the chirping of birds, there were no sounds. What was worse, the trees were all dried up and dying. In the centre of the garden was a hut. He knocked gently at the door, but getting no response, entered, to find a mendicant, deep in sleep. The prince thought it improper to disturb the old man. He came out, ate some pomegranates, and tired that he was, soon fell sleep under a shady tree.

He woke up after many hours of gentle slumber to find the mendicant still asleep. The prince felt refreshed and his limbs began to crave for activity. He ran the Persian wheel to draw water, and irrigated the whole garden. Pleased with his work, and exhausted once again, he soon fell sleep once more.

The sun had risen when he opened his eyes, but the mendicant was still sleeping. He was intrigued, and decided to stay on until his strange companion woke up.

And from then on, it became his daily practice to run the Persian wheel, water the garden, eat pomegranates, tire himself out, and sleep. Months rolled by in this way. The garden came to life, with fruit that was luscious and rosy, fat and sweet. More birds built their nests, and sang to their young ones. It was indeed a joyful sight.

Early one day, while the prince was asleep, the mendicant woke up. He had been sleeping for six months. He was astonished to see the garden flourishing. He had feared that it would die when he went into his long sleep, but it was blooming. He stood outside his hut watching and wondering. Meanwhile, the prince rose too, and seeing the mysterious mendicant up and about, went to him. Gently, the prince paid his respects, and politely he stood in front of him, looking happy and content. The mendicant understood. He smiled with satisfaction and said, 'Young man, tell me how I can reward you for your good work.' The prince was wise. Respectfully he muttered,

'God has given me enough. I have no needs.'

'No,' said the mendicant. 'Say what you would like to have—anything.'

The prince repeated respectfully, 'God has given me everything. I have enough.'

The mendicant was impatient. 'I warn you,' he growled, 'This is your third and last chance. Now say what you want and you shall get it.'

At this the prince straightened up and said, 'O kind man of God, if you must give me something, then I will have Princess Pomegranate, nothing else.'

The mendicant made a long face. He was not expecting this. But he was now bound by his word. He thought for a while, then, he went inside. In a moment he was back with a ball, which he threw. He then advised the prince to follow it, and pluck the fattest fruit of the tree under which it stopped rolling. 'Then go home without looking back, or talking to me. Princess Pomegranate will be hidden in the fruit, but do not open it before you reach home, or, the princess will disappear.'

His long journey back did not trouble him now. He was returning with success, Princess Pomegranate safely tucked in his robe, confined in the fat fruit. After many weeks of this joyful journey, he reached the outskirts of his royal city, and rested in an old garden to refresh himself before going to his palace. A suspicion suddenly lurked in his mind. He looked at the fruit, and thought that fat though it was, it was not big enough to contain a princess. The mendicant could have cheated him. If he went home and in the presence of his sisters-in-law, cut open the fruit to find only its normal juicy pearls, instead of the promised princess, his shame would be unbearable. He had nearly reached home, so what if he cut the fruit now, and checked. This seemed like a sensible thought, though he was a little nervous.

With some hesitation, he broke open the fruit, and lo and behold, a beautiful princess, clad in red from head to foot, tumbled out! She was so marvellously beautiful, that the prince could not stand the sight of her, and fainted.

Princess Pomegranate was alarmed to see him faint. Hastily she sat down by him, put his head on her knees, and started fanning him for fresh air with one end of her red garment.

As Allah would have it, the gardener's widowed daughter, an evil woman, happened to pass that way, and saw the tender sight. She recognised the prince, and at once thought that the lovely little maid in the beautiful red dress was surely Princess Pomegranate, whom the prince had gone to seek. So she went to her, and told her that her prince would not recover unless she left him alone for a while. The princess was gullible, like all beautiful people, and she agreed. The gardener's daughter took her on a round of the garden. The princess was feeling thirsty, so they went to a well which was deep and dangerous. The gardener's daughter drew a bucket of water, and the princess drank from it and was refreshed.

The gardener's daughter invited her to see the reflection of her face in the well, so that she should know if she was sufficiently and wholesomely beautiful for her prince. The princess was gullible, like all beautiful people are, and not seeing the trap, looked down at her reflection. She was perfect, and so, calmly and confidently, she straightened up again.

The gardener's daughter was cunning. She said that her dress was so enchanting and overwhelmingly gorgeous that she could not really judge precisely how beautiful she was, and would have to be in an ordinary dress to appraise her beauty correctly.

The princess, who was gullible like all beautiful people are, not seeing the trap the gardener's daughter had laid for her, exchanged her dress with the evil woman, and looked down in the well again. In a flash the gardener's daughter pushed her into the well, and rushing to the senseless prince, sat by his side, placing his head on her knees, and started fanning him with her red garment. The prince woke up.

He woke up to find an ugly woman in a beautiful red dress sitting by his side. He could have fainted again at the sight of such ugliness, but he controlled himself. He feared that this woman was Princess Pomegranate, turned ugly by the mendicant, because he had, perhaps, cut the fruit a little too soon. There was nothing he could do about it. However, he had found and brought Princess Pomegranate back, so at least he had won the bet.

The prince rose up, and went to his father. The good king was overjoyed, and to celebrate his return the city was lit up. The next day he married the ugly woman. Now, when the six sisters-in-law came to see the bride, they at once recognised their gardener's widowed daughter, now pretending to be Princess Pomegranate. They looked at each other meaningfully, saying nothing. In secret they gloated over the young prince's foolishness. After the wedding the prince lived with his ugly bride, but he could not love her.

Many weeks passed, and then a marvellously beautiful red flower was seen to be growing on a stalk that rose from the bottom of the well into which the ugly woman had pushed Princess Pomegranate. This flower was so beautiful that many people came to the garden to see it. But nobody could pluck it. The moment someone put out his hand to pick the flower, it moved away. Everyone was talking about it. The gardener's daughter also heard the story, and she became jealous. She decided to destroy the flower.

In the evening when the prince came home, she lay on her bed, groaning, pretending to be sick. 'What is the matter with you?' the prince asked her.

'I have a splitting headache,' she told him between groans.

'What will cure it?' the prince enquired anxiously.

'It will never go away,' she told him, 'not unless the flower growing out of the well is plucked, ground into a paste and applied to my forehead.'

The prince went into the royal garden, and when he bent over the well to pluck the flower, strangely enough the flower did not draw back, but swung on its stalk to reach his hand, and he was able to pluck it easily. The prince then crushed its petals and applied the paste to the forehead of the ugly woman. But this gave her a real headache, worse than any she could have pretended. And so, in agony, she threw the crushed flower out of the window when the prince was not looking.

A few days later, a charming patch of succulent greens came up just under the prince's window where the woman had thrown the crushed flower. It grew in such abundance and beauty that everybody was talking about it, but nobody could dare pluck it from the back garden of the royal palace. The gardener's daughter did not like this because she guessed that it was the princess once again, come up in a different guise. So one evening when the prince returned from his royal duties, she started groaning, and pretended that she had an acute pain in her belly. Once again the prince asked her what would cure her bellyache, and she replied that it could only be cured if the succulent green patch was cleared away.

The prince had it proclaimed that all the poor and the hungry of the city were welcome to come to the back garden of the palace and pluck the greens. They came, and in no time the patch was cleared of its lovely greens. The prince had also plucked and brought in some of the greens, and he asked the ugly woman to cook them for him. How could she refuse?

But when she put the pan on the fire, the green leaves sang out.

'Hark pan, boil us, cook us now, so we can leap up and shave the ugly woman's head.'

The ugly woman was nervous. She alone had heard the message so far. She put a great weight on the lid. But she could still hear:

'Hark pan, boil us, cook us now, so we can leap up and shave the ugly woman's head.'

It became unbearable for the woman. Hastily, she threw the pan and its contents out through the window.

But as soon as the contents of the pan touched the ground, a strange carpet of multi-coloured flowers came up and in its centre a pomegranate plant sprouted, which in a few moments turned into a fully grown tree, laden with fruit. The ugly woman was watching, and when the prince came in the evening after performing his royal duties, she started groaning and pretending to be sick with an acute pain in her chest. When, as before, he asked her what would cure her, she replied that she could be cured only if the flowers in the garden were plucked off.

Once again the prince ordered a proclamation to be made, inviting all the townspeople to come and pluck the flowers. They came, and in no time the palace ground was stripped of the wonderful carpet of flowers.

Among the people who came was a little boy, who arrived rather late, when the flowers had all gone. Nevertheless he thrust his hands in the heap of leaves and torn flower stalks in the hope of finding something worthwhile. There he found a large red pomegranate and took it to his old mother who had eaten nothing since the morning. She was much pleased. Hastily, mother and son cut open the fruit, and lo and behold! Princess Pomegranate in her charming red dress tumbled out of the fruit. The old woman and the little boy were terrified. But the princess smiled, 'Please don't be afraid. Let me stay with you and I'll help you earn a good living,' she told them.

The old woman adopted her as her daughter, and the little boy treated her as a sister. The next morning the princess made a handkerchief and embroidered a beautiful flower on it. She then told the old woman to go and sell it to the youngest prince. The prince had never seen such embroidery, and he rewarded the old woman generously. With it she bought all the food that she could ever wish to eat, and still she had money left over, which she brought back home.

From then on this became their daily practice. The princess would do some embroidery every day, and the old woman would sell it to the youngest prince. The prince was deeply impressed by the beautiful embroidery and thought that somebody who could produce such gorgeous work must be a very attractive person. When the old woman told him it was her daughter who did the embroidery, he at once asked for her hand in marriage. The old woman came home and told her daughter about it. When she showed her willingness for the match the old woman accepted the proposal. The marriage took place soon, and the bride left for the prince's palace to become his second wife.

When the prince saw his bride on their first night, he was wonderstruck. In his new bride he at once recognised the Princess Pomegranate. She told him her long story of suffering and the efforts she had made to be reunited with him. His joy knew no bounds.

The first thing the prince did the next morning was to have the gardener's wicked daughter thrown into the well, and the new couple then lived happily together for the rest of the prince's life.

The prince is now dead. Princess Pomegranate has vanished, but she is not dead. She is hiding herself in a big pomegranate somewhere in a pomegranate jungle, where an old mendicant keeps watch, in between long spells of slumber. And she is waiting for her prince.

* * * * *

The Stepbrother

A farmer had two wives; and two sons, one from each wife. The older wife was wise. Her time came early, when her son was still a child. On her deathbed she thought about his future as any loving mother would. She was sure that his stepmother would not bring him up well, so she thought of a plan whereby he would not suffer at the hands of his stepmother, and grow up properly.

She then called her rival, and requested her in humility to honour her last wish.

'What is your wish?' The other woman asked. The dying woman glibly said, 'When I die, let no one cry, because it is the Lord's wish that I die. I love my son so much that I would not like him to be given any trouble. So please let him sleep in the morning as long as he wishes. When he gets up, do not force him to bathe, or wear clean clothes, for he would like to play in the dirt. Do not send him to school and waste his childhood. Never give him fresh bread, and do let him roam with his friends in the evening until late.' She had mainly banked on her understanding of a stepmother's psychology. A stepmother would always do the reverse of what her rival wished, and she was right for she was a wise woman. The other one was a plain fool.

A few moments after she had made known her wishes, she died, which made the foolish one very happy. At night, after the burial, she thought of her rival's wish and it struck her that what she wanted for her son must be good for him. The stepmother was not willing to do what was good for her stepson, therefore, she decided to do just the reverse.

She would wake the child early, give him a good bath, fresh bread, and send him to school against his dead mother's wishes. When he returned from school, she would make him read, and never allow him to waste his time with friends in the evening.

For her own son, she adopted the wishes of her rival, hoping that this would do him good. And thus the two boys were brought up in two different ways. The stepson grew into a handsome, disciplined, learned youth, whereas her own son became a worthless, dirty, vagabond, with no dignity. The educated one had pleasing manners, which made him popular, so much so, that when the village headman died, he was elected in his place. His brother could only plough the field, and live with beasts. He worked in the sun and dust, and came home tired in the evening. He was very unhappy.

One night when dinner was over, he was particularly sulky, and reproached his brother for having the very best of life's comforts, whereas he was no better than a beast of burden, though they were sons of the same father. He now demanded that they exchange jobs, so that he too could have the taste of a better life. His mother supported him. The stepson, being very wise, and respectful to his stepmother and half-brother, willingly agreed, and handed over the charge of headman, taking the plough for himself.

Next morning he went to the farm, while his brother went to his office. Now the younger brother was illiterate, and ill-mannered, and did not know anything about the collection of land revenue on behalf of the king. He could not collect a single paisa for the treasury. He was afraid, and was running from door to door like a beggar begging for alms. Nobody would listen to him. Meanwhile, news came that the king's tax collector was in the neighbouring villages. The new headman was in a panic because he could not face him. He got up at night, stole a bullock from the cattle yard, and in the darkness, without telling anyone he left the village to try his luck elsewhere, in a place where nobody knew him.

In the evening, he stopped for rest under a shady tree. Now four thugs happened to be around, who thought of stealing his beast. They approached him like decent people.

'This beast is for sale, is it not, sir?' asked one of them.

'Yes it is,' answered the fool without thinking.

'How much are you asking for it?' said the first thug.

'What will you pay?' countered the fool.

'No, you will have to tell us first.'

'Not I,' said he, because he had no idea of its price. 'You will.'

'Well, it seems impossible. But I have a good suggestion. There's a wise old man who lives close by. He will do justice to both sides,' the thug assured the fool.

'Agreed.'

'Agreed, yes, but on the condition that his decision will be binding on both parties.'

'Agreed.' the fool muttered again.

The thugs had trapped him. 'Whosoever rejects his decision, shall have his nose and ears cut off,' said the thug with such confidence, that the fool was left with no choice.

Together they went to the wise old man, who was actually, the father of the thugs. They told him the whole story. The old thug looked at the beast carefully, then said, 'I fix its price at five rupees. That is my decision.'

The fool was stunned. It was a very good beast. He could not part with it for that meagre sum! But he was bound under pain of losing his nose and ears to accept the old man's assessment.

After pocketing the small amount of money, he left. Now he had to look for a job so he walked for many days, until he reached a big village. There he went to a rich man and offered to work for him.

This rich man was cunning and mean, like many other rich men. He agreed to give him a job. 'But there are conditions,' he said.

'What conditions?' the fool asked.

'You will have to perform the following four duties in one day. One, you will plough my whole land. Two, you have to fix a hedge around it. Three, you will hunt for me. Four, you will cook the daily meals.'

The fool, hungry and penniless that he was, agreed.

'If you fail in any one of the four assignments, I will have your nose and ears chopped off.' The rich man added.

'Agreed, Agreed,' said the fool, and his fate was sealed.

He got up early in the morning and went to the farm, where he started ploughing in real earnest. He ploughed the whole day, but he could not cover half the area. It was out of the question to fix the hedge, go hunting, and do the cooking after that.

The fool left the village the same night, but without his nose and ears.

He walked back home, wiser, and told the whole story to his wise half-brother, who was enraged. He advised him to stay at home, and eat of his earnings, while he went to take revenge on those who had been so cruel to him.

The older half-brother put on a woman's dress and went in the direction his brother had taken. He reached the very spot where his brother had rested on his first leg of the journey. The four thugs were there as expected. They thought that they had now a pretty woman to deal with. They approached him. He acted coquettish, which enchanted the thugs. The first thug came forward, and said, 'Will you come with us? We will be good to you.'

He nodded in agreement, and rose to follow them in his beautiful and rich woman's dress.

The first thug said, 'I am going to marry her.'

The second cut in, 'No. She will be my bride.'

The third added sharply, 'But she is closest to my age.'

The fourth muttered, 'I need a bride immediately.'

The first thug was clever. He did not want a quarrel in front of the fair lady. He suggested that they let their father decide. They were thugs, but respectful sons of a cunning old father. The others agreed to his suggestion, and so the whole group, with the would-be bride in tow, went to their father.

They told their father the whole story. Each son put his best foot forward in claiming the lady. The old man heard each one of them with patience, then, he gave his verdict.

'I have been a widower for a long, long time. Your mother went to Paradise when you were little children, and I will join her soon. There is very little time left for me to enjoy the world. This woman will, therefore, be mine. Now you get out of here, you puppies!' And the obedient 'puppies', disappointed as they were, left without growls or scowls.

The old man smiled at this sudden gift from Dame Fortune, and was very proud of the obedience of his sons. Then he rose to take her hand. But the wise brother suddenly tore off his woman's dress, pounced upon the old man, and beat him mercilessly. The old man cried for help, but his sons were now too far away, nursing their own wounds.

He beat him hard, and said, 'Was it not you who fixed the price of that great beast at five rupees?'

The old man pleaded with him to show mercy since he was bleeding. But the wise brother would not stop. At last the old man begged him to take all his treasures which lay buried in the corner of his courtyard, and leave him alone.

This suited the wise man. So he dug out and took all his treasures, and left.

After some time the four obedient sons returned home expecting to see their father enjoying his worldly pleasures. They were taken aback. They heard his painful story, but not without a pinch of satisfaction. But he was their father after all, so they nursed his wounds until the next morning, but he was no better. In fact, he was worse. They decided to take him to a doctor in the neighbouring village. They put him on a cot, and holding the four sides of the cot they started to walk.

After some distance they came upon a mendicant, meditating alone by the roadside. They put the cot down, and approached him respectfully. The first thug spoke:

'O wise man of God. Our old father is badly injured. Please help him.'

The wise man of God opened his eyes, looked at them searchingly, and said, 'Did someone beat him up?'

'Yes sir.' The first thug answered.

'I will treat him, if Allah wills,' said the wise man of God. 'One of you should go and fetch some water. The second should bring some gum, the third some milk. And lastly, the fourth should run and get some honey.'

And so the four loving sons of their father went in four directions. When they were away from sight, the wise old man of God rose to tear his dress away. He was the same wise brother of the fool, the old man's would-be bride. He raised his big hand, and started beating him up again.

'Did you fix the price of that great beast at five rupees?' Yes, yes, he did. The old man started crying for mercy again, but the wise brother continued hammering him until he offered him the bag of money hidden in the pillow, which he was taking for his treatment. The wise brother was actually quite kind of heart. He, therefore, took the little moneybag, and left the old man. But instead of going on his way, he hid himself in a nearby tree with a thick foliage.

In a short while, the four sons returned to see their father in a worse condition than they had left him. The old man narrated the whole story in short syllables. The four brothers were numb with fear at the cleverness of the enemy. They were so afraid that they decided to leave the area for good, for fear that their enemy would return again.

Hidden in a nearby tree, the wise brother had heard the whole conversation. He got down, and taking a short cut, was able to take a position on the road much ahead of them. He saw the party slowly coming towards him. Nearby, there was a shepherd, looking after a flock of sheep. He called him, and said, 'If you want a reward and if you can run fast, I will give you twenty rupees. Go to that party that's coming up, and yell, 'Are you now running away for fear of me?' Then run away. Here count your twenty rupees.'

The shepherd wanted easy money, who would not? And he could run fast. He counted the silver, and went up to the approaching party. He stood for a moment, then yelled,'Are you now running away for fear of me?' Having said this, he ran. The four obedient sons of their father put the cot down and ran after him in pursuit. Soon the old man was alone. Then up to him walked our wise man with his rod, and started beating up the old man mercilessly. Again the old man begged him for mercy and offered him a bag of money, the last remnant of his treasure, which he was hiding in his trousers.

The wise brother was kind of heart, and he had driven a good bargain. He had also settled his scores with the old man, and through him with the whole family. So he collected the bag, and left. Now he went in the direction of the village where the rich man lived, and where lay buried the nose and ears of his brother, the fool.

Soon he met the cunning rich man to whom he offered his services for any kind of job, and was taken on. Early the next morning, he left for the farm of the cunning rich man, with a plough and a pair of bullocks. He returned in the evening looking quite calm and content.

The rich man came home and asked him if he had done all the four jobs which he had been told to do, to which question the wise brother replied in the affirmative. This surprised his master.

'How come?' exclaimed the cunning rich man.' I want to see with my own eyes what you have done.'

'You are welcome' said the wise brother, and together they went to the farm. The cunning rich man saw that there were furrows made by the plough across the whole field. Thus the first job had been done. The rich man then looked around. On the four corners of his farm were four little hedges. The second job was done too.

Then they returned home, the rich man expected that he had not succeeded in hunting, there being no game available in the vicinity. 'Have you hunted?' inquired the cunning rich man.

'Yes, master.'

'And have you cooked the game?'

'Yes, master.

'Then serve the meal', growled the rich man. The wise brother went to the kitchen, and, in a moment, brought a dish of delicious meat, which his master sat down to eat, and ate with relish.

Now the rich man was very fond of his pet, a bitch, which used to keep him company whenever he took his meals, but which was now nowhere to be seen. He whistled for her to come. At this the wise brother informed him that he was whistling for an animal that he had already partly eaten.

'What do you mean?' roared his master.

'Well, sir, I hunted the bitch, and cooked your meal. That was your requirement, wasn't it?' said the wise brother.

'I dismiss you forthwith.' barked the rich man.

'Very well sir,' responded our hero serenely. 'You have lost the bet anyway, since I have completed all the four jobs in a single day. I will go, but just as a reminder of your benevolence I will take with me a part of your nose, and your ears, which are rather large for your face anyhow.'

The rich man had lost the bet and there was no way he could avoid paying the penalty. The wise brother was quick to do this last job, and he did it efficiently. Then he left for his village.

Walking fast he reached home in a few days. He put the nose and the ears of the rich man, and the treasures of the thugs before his foolish brother, who had now become wise.

His brother was very happy and handed over to his wise brother the job of the village headman to which, being uneducated, he himself was not at all suited. For himself he kept the rugged plough and the bullock since he had the experience, the aptitude and the talent to work with them.

* * * *

Prince Ruby

On his way home one evening, a woodcutter came upon a bush laden with red berries. His children had not tasted berries for a long time so he thought of them and started plucking the fruit. In the middle of the bush, protected by many sharp thorns, was the best, the reddest and fattest of all the berries. The woodcutter was tempted, and though the thorns bruised him badly, he managed to reach it and break it off. Then having filled his pockets with more berries, he left for home.

He was late for dinner. The children had eaten their meagre meal of bread and water and had gone to sleep. It was dark in the room, though the dim oil lamp cast ugly shadows in the courtyard. He went inside where his wife gave him food and water. He took out the berries from his pockets and unbelievingly, the room was lit up as though by a thousand wax candles. The fattest berry was the source of the most beautiful rays of light. The woodcutter and his wife were struck with wonder. They could not understand the strange phenomenon, but they were very happy. This would save them their daily oil and the large berry would give them brilliant light each night to boot. Then they went to sleep.

The next morning they gave their children their share of the fruit, saving the one that had shone. When night came, and all was dark, they placed the large berry in the middle of the room where it made brilliant light again like the night before. The woodcutter's wife was excited, like all women are over something that is unusual, and she thought that the berry must be a very precious object, fit only for a king. So she suggested to her husband that he take it to the king, and her husband agreed to do so.

Next morning the woodcutter took the berry to the king and told him the whole story. At first the king was astonished, but when he took a closer look at the berry, he found that it was not a berry at all but the rarest ruby in the world. He rewarded the woodcutter generously and sent the ruby to his queen as a gift.

The queen was very pleased with the gift and she showed it to all her ladies. But when night fell her excitement wore off. Before going to bed she tossed the precious gem carelessly under her pillow and went to sleep.

When the queen woke up the next morning she had completely forgotten the ruby. But after she had taken her bath, and put on fresh garments she thought of the gem under her pillow. Maids ran to bring it for her and she followed them to the bed, but great was their amazement when instead of the ruby under her pillow, they found a beautiful baby sitting on the bed, smiling like the rays of the morning sun. The queen had no issue, so this seemed like the answer to her prayers. The king, who was immediately sent for, was no less pleased than his queen. He ordered a royal feast to be prepared for all the people in the city. And then there was great rejoicing, for the king had been blessed with an heir after all. And what an heir! A gift straight from heaven.

By a happy coincidence, the vizir was blessed with a baby girl the same day. The child was as beautiful as a fairy. The king immediately asked for her hand for his son and it was settled there and then that they would marry each other when they grew up.

The two babies started their lives under the care of able nurses and wise teachers, and as days of peace and happiness pass faster than days of grief, Prince Ruby soon grew up into a handsome youth and the vizier's daughter became a perfect beauty. The king made a new palace for them and when it was ready, they were married. It has passed down to us from our ancestors, who were present on the occasion, that the pomp and splendour of that marriage is a story that few mortals can do justice to. In short, it was the most befitting wedding for two beautiful people.

With all his dreams realised, and desires fulfilled, the king died, leaving the throne to his son, Prince Ruby.

The prince was popular as a ruler, and was a loving husband as well. Life was beautiful for the young royal couple. One day, an old hag, with a pitcher over her head, came to the palace gate and sent word to the princess that she sold the most wonderful curds in the world. Since the princess had not eaten curds for a long time, she had the old woman called in. It so happened that Prince Ruby entered her chambers at the same time. He looked sternly at the old hag, and ordered her to leave the palace, and she left without saying a word. Then he looked at his wife and told her that in her own interest, she must never see the old hag again. The princess did not understand and the prince did not explain the matter any further. He simply got up and left.

Many days passed and everybody forgot the old hag; but she came again. This time she was dressed as a bangle seller, and was carrying a basket of glass bangles. At the palace gate she sent word that she had brought glass bangles in colours that nobody had ever seen. She was called in.

The bangles really had the most unusual colours anybody had ever seen, and their glass was so delicate and clear that only a princess could afford to buy them.

The old hag started helping the princess wear the bangles but she saw to it that in doing so each one of them was broken. Soon all her bangles were small broken pieces of colourful glass, and the princess a dismayed woman. Noticing the princess' unhappiness, she asked her a straight question.

'Who is your husband? He must be a demon by blood, otherwise all the bangles could not have broken like this.'

'No, no, he is human, son of the old king,' replied the princess.

'What is his caste?' The old hag insisted.

'Well, he is a prince; that is his caste,' said the princess confidently. But the old hag had a plan. Stubbornly she asked, 'Does he or does he not keep you at a distance at night?'

Now the fact was that he did keep her at a distance. When he ate with the princess, he always drew a line in the middle of the dish. When he slept with her, he kept a naked sword between them. But she had never thought about it. Now that the old hag had brought this up, it occurred to her that he did indeed keep a distance, and she said so. Having done her mischief, the old hag left. The princess started thinking gloomily about her husband.

When the prince came home after doing his day's work, she asked him about his caste. The prince was shaken. He tried to ward off the question, but the casualness of his answer made the princess suspect him all the more and she insisted on knowing the truth. The prince shouted at her and tried to close the subject, but alas, when the cobra of doubt raises its head in someone's heart, it poisons the whole being. It had bitten the princess.

Many days passed. The princess kept crying, which made the prince very unhappy. He went to her again and tried to calm her down. She saw this as her chance, so she threatened him that she would kill herself with the deadliest of poisons if he did not tell her his caste. Now this is a very compelling device, always effective, and always certain to make a man weak. He promised to answer her question in the morning.

The next morning the prince woke up early, for he too had had a sleepless night on account of fears known only to him. He went to the princess and for the last time, warned her not to insist on her question or she would repent. But she would not listen to him.

Finding no way of succeeding with the princess, he calmed himself and led her out of the palace. They did not speak to each other and walking silently, they reached the bank of a river where they stopped. The prince once again warned the princess that she would repent if she did not drop her question, but she was an ill fated, obstinate woman.

The prince entered the river, and walked deeper into it. When the water came up to his neck, he looked at her with pleading eyes, in the hope that she would finally understand. But fate had blinded her judgement. She was adamant. Then, in the twinkling of an eye, the prince dipped into the water and disappeared. A few bubbles rose, and a moment after, a cobra raised its head precisely where the prince had drowned himself. Looking at the princess the snake said to her, 'O princess, I did everything to stop you from asking me my caste, and I warned you that you might be sorry if you insisted, but you did not listen to me. Now hear me: My name is Raja Hari Tarang, the son of the king of snakes. I left home after a quarrel with my father and lived first with a woodcutter, in the form of a ruby. I then reached the king's palace, where I decided to turn into a man. The old hag who visited you was a witch, sent by my grandfather in search of me. That is why I had forbidden you to meet her, but you did not listen to me. Now I must go back to where I belong, leaving you alone.' Having said this, the snake disappeared into the deep waters.

The princess now realised her terrible mistake. She cried and waited, but it was useless. She came back to her palace.

After she lost her prince she was in so much anguish that she could not get a wink of sleep. Nights were long in those days, and parted lovers found them even longer. When affairs of the state began to suffer from neglect, the grand vizir decided to do something about bringing his daughter back to normalcy. He had it proclaimed throughout the kingdom that any person who could tell the princess a previously untold story every night, would be rewarded with a gold coin for each story. Storytellers flocked to the palace but as everybody knows from sad experience, there are few untold stories in this world. So nobody could really help the princess.

At long last an old man came to the palace, claiming that he could tell such a story. He was immediately ushered into the princess' chambers.

Having settled himself comfortably on the carpet, he spoke thus:

'Being a very poor man, unable to earn enough for my family, I once decided to try my luck in distant lands. So, taking leave of my people, I set out one fine morning, taking the North road. I did not know my destination and I depended on Allah's guidance alone. When night fell, I found myself in the depths of a dark and cruel jungle. Cold and alone, with nothing to eat, and surrounded by beasts, I was afraid. So I decided to spend the night on a tree. Finding a tall one, I climbed it and sat on a branch, with my back resting against the tree trunk. I could not sleep but I dozed until the middle of the night, when I saw a spectacle which no human being had ever seen before.' Having said this much, the old storyteller begged to take leave.

The princess was interested. She asked, 'But what was that spectacle?' 'We shall keep that for tomorrow, my princess. I cannot tell that now,' said the old man and he got up, and started putting on his shoes. The princess gave him a gold coin and promising to complete his story on the following night, he left.

He was a good old man, though a bit greedy, which has been the nature of all old men through the ages. He came again as promised and resumed his unfinished story thus:

'In the middle of the night, when I was dozing, I heard the hiss of snakes. I opened my eyes and looked down from my perch. I saw two of them, right under the tree. Then, before my very eyes, they turned into human beings. They collected some wood and made a huge fire. Having done that, they again became snakes and crawled away. I was wondering at this strange happening when in a moment, I saw another snake coming towards the tree under which the fire now roared. He too turned into a man and making a broom out of some bushes, started sweeping the ground. Having done this, he went back to his original form and crawled away. I was wondering at this strange happening, when a third snake came and like the others, took human form. There was a lot of dust from the sweeping, and it rose high up into my eyes. He brought some water from a nearby spring and started sprinkling the ground with it. The dust soon settled. Having done this he became a snake again and disappeared. Now I wondered no more; I had begun to expect other marvels. Soon I saw two more snakes. They came and after turning human, they spread the finest Kashmir carpets, and left. They were followed by two more snakes, who placed a throne under the tree. It was made of gold and studded with rubies, and shone even brighter than the fire.

It was like the world of dreams; quite fantastic, my princess. And may you rule the realms of the seven seas as long as the stars keep their light and day follows night. As for me, I am an old man, tired and sleepless. I cannot continue telling this story to-night.'

He rose to put on his shoes. The princess was deeply interested in the story and gave him two gold coins instead of one, so that he would return the next night, to complete his story.

He was a good old man, though a bit greedy, and the two gold coins, instead of one, suited him doubly. He kept his word and returned early next evening. He then took up the thread of his story and continued thus:

'Having put down the throne, they left as I told you. All was quiet for a while, then more snakes started coming from all four directions. They would come, take human form, and sit respectfully on the rugs. In a few moments they had formed a court which sat quietly waiting for the king to arrive.

Then a huge cobra came hissing. On his two sides were smaller cobras, which formed a procession. On the head of the big cobra, sat comfortably, a small golden cobra. All the courtiers stood up to welcome the newly arrived party.

In a moment, all the newcomers turned into human beings. The big cobra became a grand old man and with a natural crown over his head, he was distinguishable as the king. He sat on the throne. The golden cobra on his head who had turned into a beautiful young prince jumped into the lap of the king, his grandfather, and sat there.

When the court had settled down, a party of the finest dancing girls arrived, and in the midst of heavenly music and tinkling of golden bells, they presented one dance after another. All were rapt while this lasted, but moments of happiness like moments of misery are short-lived, so when the morning star was left alone on the sky, the dancing girls left. The court did likewise, respectfully and in an orderly fashion. Turning into snakes, they silently crawled away before the break of day.

When all had left, the golden prince stood alone, looking south. In the end, he uttered, 'You have found out my caste, princess, and are now in misery. But I am having the best of times. Thus have you sealed the bargain yourself. Thus will it for ever be'. Having uttered these words, he turned into a golden snake again, and slid away in the darkness of the jungle.

I was the only witness of this most unusual happening. I was afraid, and anxiously awaited the first rays of the sun. They seemed to me so desirable and priceless that night! The night was ebbing. Its back was already broken, and in a few moments the golden rays of the sun lit the jungle. I never went to that place again, and never told this story to anyone.'

The princess was so excited and so pleased with the story that she ordered that the man's mouth be filled with rubies. Her orders were carried out immediately. Then she ordered that an elephant load of gold coins be sent to his house, which also was done. The princess was certain that the golden prince in the lap of his grandfather was her husband, the Raja Hari Tarang who had disappeared in the river waters. She wanted to go there herself with the old storyteller.

The old man was a good sort, though a bit greedy, and since he expected an even bigger reward next time, he immediately agreed to lead the princess to the jungle.

The old man and the princess set out early in the morning, and when night fell, reached the exact spot, where the tall tree stood as before. They climbed it, and hiding themselves in the foliage of its branches, waited.

Midnight was slow in coming like all things you wait for, but it came. As before, with midnight came the snakes. First they made a fire, then they swept the floor and spread it with beautiful Kashmir carpets. Then the courtiers started coming and settling down on the carpets. Last to come was the king cobra's procession. The king occupied his throne, and his grandson sat on his huge knees. Then the dancing girls presented their dances and played music. Everybody was enjoying themselves until, with the morning star, they left. The last to go was our prince, Raja Hari Tarang, the husband of the forlorn princess. He stood up alone and uttered, 'You have found out my caste, O princess, and are in misery because of it, while I am having the best of everything. Thus shall it be forever.' Having said this, he was about to lie down in order to become a snake, when the princess jumped down, and grabbing a corner of his robe said, 'Don't go away like this, my prince, I beg of you!' 'The prince was flabbergasted. Then he understood, and admonished her, 'But it is your own choosing, my princess. Leave me alone, for if my grandfather gets a whiff of you he will blow you into ashes with one breath.'

But the princess was firm, and as it is sometimes necessary to be firm, she held on to his robe until the prince became helpless. He actually loved her, and love makes people helpless, as you surely know, wise reader.

He told her that there was only one way she could get him back, and advised her thus:

'Come early in the evening tomorrow, with a cauldron full of milk, boiled and sweet. Then stand under the tree waiting for the party to arrive. Do not be afraid for no harm shall come to you. Wait until the dance and music make my grandfather happy. Then come forward and start serving milk to the party, approaching my grandfather last of all, for he likes to feed his subjects first. Your hospitality will make my grandfather very tender and kindly disposed towards you. Then he will ask you to say what you want. But do not say what you want, for if you do, he will blow you up into ashes with the poison of his breath. Say, 'What God has given me is enough,' and stand respectfully. He will ask you again to say what you want, but you must respond as before. At this his generosity will find itself challenged and he will be provoked. He will ask you a third time, a bit angrily though, to say what you want. At this, stand erect, and say respectfully that first you want his word of honour that he will give you what you want and not harm you. He will willingly give you his word. Once he has promised, say that you want me. And now that the eastern horizon is turning red, it is time for me to go. 'Good-bye my princess, and may God show you the way,' saying this, the prince turned into a cobra and crawled away.

The princess went to her capital and returned with a cauldron full of milk, sweet and boiled. She did not forget to also bring a number of cups, made of gold, which she washed and neatly arranged under the tree before nightfall.

When night fell, she stood there alone, waiting for her only chance to recover her husband.

At the appointed time the party arrived as usual, and the dance and music put the old king in a happy mood. This was her moment. She went forward with cups of milk, and started serving them. She approached the good king last of all. As the result of her hospitality the king became warmly and kindly disposed towards her, and asked her to say what she would like to have for a reward.

'Sire, God has given me enough' was her reply.

'No, say what you want, I ask you.' The king of the snakes insisted.

'Sire, God has given me enough' was her reply again.

'I ask you for the last time'. The king said, and then thundered, 'Say what you want!'

At this the princess stood erect but spoke respectfully, 'Have I the king's word, that whatever I ask for will be granted?'

'Yes,' said the king, 'whatever you ask for, will be granted'. At this the princess looked at the prince at his knees, and said firmly, 'Give me the prince, your grandson, I want him for my reward'.

The king was taken aback, for he did not expect this, He loved his grandson above everything else in the world, but not above his word of honour, for he was a proud king, like kings used to be in the olden days. But he was frustrated and enraged all the same.

'If you had not taken my word of honour, I would have blown you into ashes with one single breath, but you are a very clever girl. I love my grandson, whom I have found after twenty-five years. His father, my son had died, and I was to hand over my vast empire to him. But alas! This was not fated.' Tears rolled down and wet his white beard. He kissed the forehead of his grandson and handed him over to the princess. That night, the court was dismissed early.

The princess returned home happily with her prince, and handing over the charge of the kingdom to him, settled herself to becoming a good wife, which is never to be too inquisitive and never demanding to know the secrets of one's husband.

* * * * *

The Precious Handkerchief

In olden days, there lived a poor young man, who could not make a living for himself, though he toiled all day. He had no family and no other ties. He decided to go to some other kingdom to try his luck and raise a family.

He left his town early in the morning and started walking without a particular destination in mind, hoping to reach some city which would change his luck. He walked all day, and when night came, he found himself in the midst of a jungle, where it seemed dangerous to sleep. He was thinking about it, when suddenly, unexpectedly, he heard sweet music in the jungle. Hoping that he was close to a human habitation, he started walking in the direction from which the music came.

After some distance, he found himself before a group of fairies, who were singing and dancing for a group of demons under an old banyan tree. He was afraid to move or to speak, so he hid himself behind a tree and began to watch.

He watched the frolics of the fairies and demons for God knows how long, until he observed the morning star, brilliant and alone in the sky, which indicated that night was now over. The fairies and demons started leaving and soon there was no one left. He thanked God, and when the first rays of the sun shone, he came out of hiding, and went closer to the venue of the party in order to observe it better. He was extremely pleased to find a handkerchief there, which was superb in every way. Some fairy had carelessly dropped it.

He decided to return home and make a present of this unique handkerchief to the king, who would surely reward him handsomely for it.

He went back home and presented the handkerchief to the king who was very pleased with him and rewarded him with an elephant load of rubies.

This king had two queens. He respected the older of the two more than he loved his younger queen, and he, therefore, sent the handkerchief to the older queen. She showed it to her rival, who became very jealous.

At night, when the king came to the younger queen's chambers, he found her lying in an old cot, crying her heart out. And she threatened to kill herself, unless, she too had an identical handkerchief. The king loved her, for she was young and beautiful. He promised to procure one for her too.

Next morning he summoned the poor beggar who had now got an elephant load of rubies, and ordered him to find another, identical handkerchief for the younger queen, or he would he trampled under the feet of the royal elephants.

There was no escape for the poor beggar. He, therefore, begged for a year's leave in which to carry out the king's orders. His request was granted.

He left the city, and went straight to the place where he had seen fairies dancing for the demons, and he hid himself behind a tree. He waited and waited but all was quiet until night turned into day. Yet no one came.

He was utterly dismayed and since to go back to the king without the handkerchief would mean death under the feet of the royal elephants, he decided to go on to some other kingdom, where he could live in peace.

After walking for many days, he arrived at the outskirts of a city. It was already night, and he needed food and rest. He, therefore, knocked at the door of the first house that he saw.

In response to his knocking, an old woman came out, lantern in hand. She was a kind and gentle old woman. She took him in, gave him food, and a bed to sleep on. After filling his stomach, when he stretched himself out on the bed, he noticed that the old woman was weeping in a corner. He was about to ask her the reason for her grief when the old woman started laughing. This puzzled him even more. He sat up and asked the old woman what was the matter with her.

The old woman tried to avoid answering his question, but upon his insistence she told him that she was laughing because eight days from then her son was to get married, and she would bring home a beautiful daughter-in-law. And she was crying because the night after that it would be her son's turn to be eaten by a demon who visited the city every day and for whose repast the king had ordered one young man from the city to be given up each day as a daily offering.

The poor traveller was disgusted with his life. He did not want to live such a destitute life, and at the same time, wished to do a good turn to the old woman. He offered to go to the demon instead of her son.

The old woman did not agree at first, but motherhood being selfish, she finally agreed to the proposal. She told him the exact place where the demon would meet him, and giving him a good sword and a lot of useless wishes, sent him to the appointed place. In a short while he was there. The demon had not yet arrived.

Then, while he stood and wondered, a storm arose, bringing rain and hail; and in the lightning and thunder, the demon came flying over a cloud, shouting 'man smell, man smell'.

The young man stood fearlessly. The demon looked at him with some respect, because he was used to seeing his victims cowering and cringing in great fear. He stood for a moment and then, laughing loudly, extended his enormous hand to grab his neck. Upon this, the young man gave him such a powerful blow with his sword, that his hand was chopped off, and fell with a thud, a bucket of blood gushing out of it. The demon had been taken by surprise, and in great pain and confusion, he ran for his life.

The young man took the hand of the demon to show to the king, who gave him a handsome reward for his bravery. This he gave to the old woman.

He spent a few more days in that city to make sure that the demon did not return. And the demon did not return to torment the unfortunate population again. All was now well. He, therefore, took leave of the old woman and resumed his travels.

He walked and walked, and ultimately, when night was falling, he came to the outskirts of a city. He was hungry and tired and badly needed food and rest.

He did not know anybody in the place he was, and so he knocked at the first house. An old woman answered his call, lantern in hand.

She gave him food and a bed, and after he had finished eating, when he was about to sleep, he observed that the old woman laughed when she came into the room, and cried, when she went out of the room. He was perplexed.

He asked the old woman what was the matter with her, to which she replied that she smiled, because her son was to be married in eight days, and she cried, because the following day it was his turn to be eaten by a she-demon who visited the city each night.

The young man offered to go in place of her son. She hesitated at first but motherhood being selfish, she agreed and explaining everything to him, sent him away with a good sword and a lot of useless wishes.

The young man reached the place where the she-demon was expected, but she had not yet arrived. Then, while he stood there waiting, a storm arose, bringing rain and hail, lightning and thunder, during which the she-demon came flying over a cloud, shouting, 'Man-smell, Man-smell'.

The young man stood fearlessly. The she-demon looked at him with some respect and then laughing loudly, extended her great big hand to grab his neck.

This was the moment he was waiting for, and he thrust the sword at her. But the she-demon was agile. She jumped aside and the sword fell on her dress, cutting off a piece from it.

The she-demon had not been prepared for an attack and she thought that this was no ordinary mortal. Her heart filled with fear; she jumped on her cloud and was gone in a flash.

He took the piece of the she-demon's dress to show to the king, who gave him a handsome reward for frightening the evil creature out of her wits. The she-demon never came back to the city after that.

A few days later, he left the city, taking with him the hand of the demon and the piece of the she-demon's garment. He had to find the fairies of the handkerchief.

He walked and walked in the jungle without hope of reaching his destination until one day at noon, when the sun was ablaze and his tongue scorched and dry, he reached a well, close to which was a beautiful golden palace.

When he went close to the well, he was surprised to see a beautiful girl in a gorgeous dress, who gave him a smiling welcome at first, and then started to cry. The young man was puzzled.

When he questioned her, she told him that he was treading the land of the demons where she was a prisoner. She had smiled when she saw him because it was twelve years since she had seen a human being. She had cried because her captor the demon would make a morsel of him when he came home with his she-demon wife from their hunt.

The young man did not show any fear. This encouraged the girl, who was a princess, stolen by the demon from her garden when she was a child. She took the young man home and before the arrival of the demon and his wife, she hid him behind a curtain.

When they came home, the girl served them a sumptuous dinner which gave them great pleasure. The she-demon told her husband that the girl had grown up and that he should be now looking for a match for her, instead of wasting his time like a foolish old demon. The demon agreed that it was a sensible idea and said that he would like to marry her to the young man who had chopped off his hand, for he was truly brave.

The she-demon did not agree. She insisted that the young man, who had cut a piece of her dress, was truly brave, and that she would like to make him her son-in-law.

Upon this the two began to quarrel and shout at each other. The princess, their adopted daughter, now came forward and said that if they promised to spare her life and of their would-be son-in-law, she would satisfy both of them. They did not understand her at all, but they agreed to do as she wished, for they loved her.

Upon this, the princess brought out the young man from behind the curtain, to the joyful surprise of the two, who willingly agreed to take him for their son-in-law, as he satisfied both of them. Straightaway they arranged the wedding and the two were married then and there.

The next morning the young couple sought their leave to go and live with the humans, so that they could produce children and bring them up among their own kind.

The old demons were now very sorry, but what could they do before the wishes of their son-in-law? As everybody knows, after one gives one's daughter away to a young man, one has to become mute. The demons had no choice.

At the parting they gave the girl the best jewels in the world and bales of silk which the fairies had woven with their own hands. It was a dowry that no king has given even his most beloved daughter.

The young man was overjoyed on seeing the silk bales for it was the same cloth as was used for the handkerchief of the fairies, which he was looking for to give to his king. Now he could make as many handkerchiefs as he wished.

He reached his city in great pomp and splendour, and went straight to the court with his bride. He offered the king a whole bale of silk with which to make handkerchiefs. The king accepted his gift, and then looked at the bride. He rose from his seat in joyful surprise at seeing the girl, because she happened to be his daughter, who had been stolen as a child from his palace garden by an unknown demon, and had lost all hope of seeing again.

* * * * *

The Wise Pigeon

In olden times, there lived a good king, who was ageing without having been blessed with a male heir to whom he could hand over his empire, which he had managed so well. He prayed endlessly, and so did the queen, his only wife, to invoke God's mercy. The city beggars were given ample alms, and the holy men of God were served well, in the hope that they would pray for him. At long last, when he was near the end of his life, his hair turned grey, and his eyesight weak, the prayers of the holy men bore fruit, and he was blessed with a son with a face more beautiful than the moon.

Rejoicings at the birth of his son over, the king thought of betrothing his son to the daughter of another good king straightaway, because he was at the end of his days, and expected to die soon. He was afraid that once he was not there to give his son the benefit of his wisdom and experience, the young man was apt to make the wrong choice in the selection of a wife. He, therefore, despatched wise emissaries to the four corners of the earth to make an appropriate selection for the future wife of his son.

The wisest of his emissaries went the farthest, crossing seven seas, where he met his king's exact equal in everything. This king had a little baby daughter, more beautiful than the flower fairies. This was what the emissary was looking for. The match was settled more eagerly by the father of the girl because it has always been hard to find proper matches for girls, and the fathers of marriageable girls understand this very well.

Having settled the marriage, and taken presents for his king, the emissary returned to his king across the seven seas. He had also fixed the date of the marriage, which was eighteen years hence, in the second moon of spring.

After a long voyage, the emissary finally returned to his king and told him about his find. The king was overjoyed.

The emissary was rewarded generously and the whole city was entertained to a sumptuous feast at which succulent chicken and mutton, sweet-smelling long-grained rice, luscious fruits and mouth-watering sweets were served in abundance.

The king started counting the days for the marriage of his son, who was still a baby. But he was old and his counting was not very good. Besides, he died soon.

The grand vizir was mean and treacherous, and he hatched a plan whereby he would have the baby prince murdered, and capture the throne. But among conspirators there are sometimes loyal servants of God, who will never allow events to take their evil, cruel course. One such God-fearing soul reported the plot to the queen mother. Afraid for the life of her infant son, the queen who was now alone and friendless, wrapped him in her shawl and stole out of the city at dead of night.

After travelling for many days she reached a kingdom where nobody knew her. Her dress in rags, her shoes torn, her face hardened by the sun and wind, she looked like a common beggar. But her nine hundred thousand rupees worth necklace still hung round her throat. She was hungry, and she decided to sell it. She went to a jeweller. On looking at her necklace, he suspected her of being a thief. But when she told him her story, his heart melted. He welcomed her as a sister, and asked her to live with him. She accepted his hospitality and the prince started growing up under his new uncle's care, in a manner befitting a prince.

In the same city there lived a *shikari*[1] who used to spread a net into which he trapped birds for a living. One day, some wild pigeons who were flying overhead saw the grains scattered on the ground for bait. They could not see the net and so they decided to descend. Among them was an old pigeon, the wisest of them all, who advised them against it. But they were young, and what is more, they were hungry. They thought that the old pigeon was only a fool. So they ignored his warning and descended one after the other, with the old pigeon following them helplessly. They were all caught in the clever *shikari's* net, the old pigeon included. Now they repented, but in vain.

Thereupon they requested the old pigeon to find a way out for them. He thought for a while and then said, 'Yes, there is a way. All of you should become absolutely motionless and pretend to be dead. If you do that, the *shikari* will be taken in, and believing you to be of no use to him, he will throw each of you out. Wait until you are all thrown away and continue to pretend to be dead until the last bird is safely out of the net. Then fly away together'.

They did what he suggested. The *shikari* took them for dead, and thinking that the grains were poisonous, he started throwing each one of them away in dismay. They started counting. In the middle of the count, an ant bit the *shikari* and he jumped up. The pigeons had their eyes closed, and were counting only the sound made by each pigeon as it was thrown away and hit the ground. The sound of the *shikari* jumping gave them the impression that another pigeon had fallen, and they went wrong by one. The *shikari* had thrown all but one, the old wise pigeon, when they thought that they were all out of the net. So they flew away before the old pigeon could be released. The *shikari* now understood the trick they had played on him but there was nothing he could do. He, therefore, decided to take his revenge on the wise old pigeon. He took him home and asked his daughter to slaughter and cook him.

When the pigeon heard this terrible command, he begged the man to spare his life, and in return he would help him make a fortune. But the *shikari* was not prepared to trust him, having been cheated once. The pigeon begged him to give him one chance. He told the man to carry him in a cage to the city square, and make a bid to sell him, albeit, letting him settle the price with the customer.

The *shikari* did what he suggested. He stood in the city square, cage in hand. After a short time, our prince who had now grown up, came and asked the price. The *shikari* told him to ask the pigeon. Surprised though he was, the prince did what the man suggested. The pigeon told him that his price was four diamonds, which the prince immediately produced from his pocket. The pigeon suggested that two of the gems be handed over to the *shikari*, and the remaining two be tied under his wings; it was done.

The prince went home happy with his bargain. At home he found his mother very unhappy that day, so he went to her and asked her what the matter was. She told him gloomily that if he had not lost his empire, they would have now been preparing for his marriage with the daughter of the king, across the seven seas, which his father had settled before he died. But alas! it was now just a dream.

The prince said nothing. He came back to the pigeon who noticed his grief. The pigeon secretly smiled, because he knew that the marriage was possible still. He talked to the prince and said that in a certain jungle, there lived a flying horse. 'Go find that horse and we shall fly to the kingdom of your father-in-law, in time for the wedding.'

The prince set out in search of the horse, with the pigeon perched on his arm. They found the horse and riding on its back, ordered it to fly to the kingdom across the seven seas. After several days when they descended in the capital city of the kingdom, they found great jubilation and gaiety. They soon learnt the reason for this festivity, which was that the king's daughter was to be wedded that day. The prince found this difficult to face. He was worried about his mother, who wanted that princess for a daughter-in-law, and would be badly hurt if the princess were wedded to someone other than her own son. The pigeon told the prince not to waste time. He advised him to fly to the palace of the bride. They ordered the horse to take them there and soon found themselves on the roof of the palace.

The pigeon advised the prince to wait, while he managed to bring the bride to the palace roof. Then he flew into the bridal chamber, where the princess was being dressed up for her wedding. The pigeon went close to the bride. She was excited at the bird's friendliness and tried to catch him. This was according to the pigeon's plan, who hopped back a little, and the princess was obliged to advance a little. Thus, withdrawing little by little, he took her up the stairs, and out on the roof of the palace where she came face to face with the prince.

The girl was stunned at the young man's beauty. The prince told her that he was the one to whom she had been betrothed in her infancy, and for proof, he had brought the ring that her father had sent to his father. Satisfying herself that the prince was her real fiancé, she rode behind him on the flying horse and together they flew away. They forgot the pigeon in their excitement, but he flew behind them and soon caught up with them. As usual, he perched on the prince's shoulder.

Homeward they flew, over the seven seas. Home was far and the journey long and tiring but they went on anyway. After some days their provisions were consumed, but it did not worry them, for the jungle below was laden with fresh fruit and they could see tiny rivers, full of cool, sweet water, shining in the golden sun like small snakes. They descended to eat and drink and to rest for a while. When they had eaten their fill, the princess felt sleepy. The prince was also tired, so they selected a good spot and with their elbows under their heads for pillows, went to sleep immediately. The pigeon also dozed with his head in his feathers.

A fresh breeze was blowing and they were having a very peaceful nap; but misfortune was wide awake. A sudden great flood in the river inundated the jungle. Before they could wake up and think they were swept away in different directions.

The prince caught hold of an uprooted tree and clung to it. But soon he fainted. He floated about on the surface of the water for many days, until a woodcutter in a far off land, saw him and rescued him.

When the prince came to and tried to collect his thoughts he found everything very frustrating. Nobody understood him and finding that there was nothing that he could do, he decided to stay on with the woodcutter for the rest of his life. He had no desire left for going home without his bride.

The days went by slowly, without any happy changes—in fact, without any change at all. He had no idea that the princess, his bride, who had been rescued by a washerman, was now living not too far away as the washerman's adopted daughter.

The pigeon had a different story. He had been hit by a rolling wave and injured but he managed to keep his senses. After a few days, when the flood receded, he lay on the wet grass, hungry and weak.

Then it so happened that on that sunny day, a flock of pigeons flew over the jungle. When they saw him lying helplessly, they decided to help. They took him to their abode and gave him food and water. He rested, and in a few days his strength returned, but he preferred to stay at home and meditate.

The princess never lost hope because no woman ever does. She knew that if she could find the old pigeon, she would be sure to meet the prince again. So she made a special feed which the old pigeon had taught her during their journey, just to while away the time. She prepared a large dish of that feed and placed it on the roof of the washerman's house, hoping that the old pigeon might find it and come to her.

One day the flock of pigeons which looked after the old pigeon happened to pass by, and finding more food than they had ever found at one place, descended. They ate their fill and then, taking small bits of the feed in their claws, they flew home to give it to the old pigeon. Then they told him where they had found it.

The old pigeon looked at it, and smiled for the first time in many days. Finally, he had located the princess. He flew over and met the princess, now pale and sad and living as a poor washerman's daughter. The old friends wept, their tears rolling down their cheeks like so many pearls. It was a moving scene.

The pigeon was so overwhelmed that he refused to wait for a moment more than was necessary and flew away in search of the prince.

He flew on and on, looking carefully into the vales and meadows of the area, and into the cities. At long last, after many days, he saw a young man in rags, axe in hand, cutting wood in a forest. This was his prince, and he went and sat on his shoulder.

The prince was overjoyed at seeing his friend again so unexpectedly.

The pigeon told him the story of the princess and how anxious she was to be back with him. The prince's happiness at the news was great, marred only by the thought that he could not meet the princess wearing the rags that were the only garment he had. But the pigeon laughed at his worries and reminded him of the two diamonds which he had got him to tie under his wings when the prince had bought him. The diamonds were still there, safely tucked under his wings.

All the problems thus solved, they went to the city, singing and rejoicing, and bought a handsome new outfit for the prince. But the biggest obstacle still remained. They could not get to the princess without the flying horse, which was lost too.

Once again the old pigeon undertook a long journey, this time to look for the horse. He found it in the stable of a landlord, so he flew back to the prince to give him the good news and tell him its whereabouts. Then they went back together.

The prince met the landlord and offered to buy the horse. The landlord was happy at the offer because the horse had not allowed anybody near it and so was quite useless for him. The prince bought the horse straightaway, and jumping on its back flew away with the pigeon.

They found the princess in no time. She rode behind her prince now for the journey home, after saying good-bye to her kind old adoptive father who wept at the parting. Soon the prince was back with his mother, along with the daughter-in-law she had longed for.

The same night messengers arrived from the kingdom of the prince's deceased father, which had been usurped by the treacherous grand vizir. They brought the news that the usurper had died a miserable and issueless death, and the kingdom was now looking for the prince, its rightful master.

The prince rode in state with his bride, his mother and the good old jeweller, and in the midst of great rejoicing, took over the reins of his kingdom. He proved to be a just and magnanimous ruler.

After some time when the prince was settled as king, the wise old pigeon took leave of him so that he could be with his own kind in his last days. The pigeon advised all the other pigeons never to be late in returning home, and that explains why every pigeon, however far from the nest he may be during the day, returns home before nightfall to be with his kith and kin.

* * * * *

NOTE

1. *Shikari*: Hunter

Four Friends

In days gone by there lived a cattle herder whose sole aim in life was to look after his livestock, and make a decent living for his children. For some reason he incurred the wrath of the king who ordered him to leave the country, even though he had committed no crime to earn this punishment. Now a king being a king, you cannot argue with him once he has made up his mind. So the man left the kingdom the next morning, along with his herd of cattle.

On hearing the news of his exile, his friend, the carpenter followed him, saying that life was no good without friends, and it is worthwhile to sink or swim with a friend. A third friend, a scholar, too went with them on the same plea and a fourth, a prince, who was a friend of the scholar, followed suit.

The herder, the carpenter, the scholar, and the prince, all four men set out east. After they had left their homeland behind they travelled on, without a particular destination in mind. Not knowing what unexpected situations they may have to face, they decided to find out more about each other and learn if their fellow travellers possessed any special talents that could come in handy during their wanderings.

Said the herder, 'I have no special talent, but I can tell the ancestry of man or beast to seven generations before him'. The carpenter said, 'I can make a flying divan, if I get the wood that I require.'

The scholar said, 'I know prayers which can raise a man from the dead, even if just his bones are available.'

The prince said, 'I have no particular talent, but I can fight well and destroy an enemy.'

As they were talking, a tiger came charging at them. The three friends looked at the prince and said that it was time for him to use his talent. The prince drew his sword and cut the tiger into two halves. But even in his death throes the tiger put out a paw and struck the prince in his stomach, digging with his claws into his guts. The prince fell dead at the same time as the tiger.

The herder and the carpenter said to the scholar that the time for him to prove his talent had come. The scholar put a sheet of cloth over the dead body of the prince and muttered some prayers. The prince was soon back on his feet.

Now it was seen that the prince had no talent even for his own defence. They advised him to stay where he was, as the journey ahead was going to be dangerous. The prince agreed to stay in the jungle. When his friends left, the prince felt very lonely. He started strolling about aimlessly. It was a thick and dark forest and it was unlikely that anybody lived there. But Allah was merciful and in a short time, the prince noticed smoke rising from a part of the forest. Excited, he went in the direction of the smoke, and found that it was coming from the chimney of a house. He entered the house. It was a large and beautiful mansion, and in the centre of the main room, was a beautiful young princess, sitting quietly. The princess saw him, and when he came close, she at first smiled and then wept. The prince was perplexed.

He asked the princess to explain her queer behaviour. The princess replied that she had smiled because she had seen a human being after many years; she had wept because she was the captive of a demon who would come and in no time make a meal of him.

The prince consoled her, and hid himself behind a curtain, sword in hand, waiting for the demon to arrive. The demon was not late in coming. In a few moments, he arrived shouting 'Man-smell, man-smell! Who came here in my absence?'

The princess cunningly said, 'None at all, I am the only one who's been here'. The demon did not believe her. He started looking around. The prince was watching, and when he found his moment, he chopped the demon's head off with a powerful blow of his sword. The princess embraced him with joy. Soon they married and started living in that house as man and wife.

In a few days, Allah showed mercy and the princess became a mother, which endeared her further to her prince.

The happy couple used to go out in the afternoon to a nearby rivulet, for the pleasure of watching its gentle flow. One day a shoe of the princess fell into the water and was swept away. Studded with jewels and pearls, this was a priceless shoe, which the demon had brought her as a gift.

The shoe floated far away, to a city where a washerman was washing the king's clothes. He caught it and brought it to the king. The king was hugely pleased but now he wanted the other shoe too. He called the cleverest hags of his kingdom and asked one, 'What is your special talent? The first hag replied, 'Your Majesty, I can go to the sky, but I cannot return'. 'Be off you fool', shouted the king, 'And yours?' he asked pointing to the second old hag.

The second old hag said, 'Your Majesty, I can go to the sky, and return, and tear a part of it, but I cannot stitch it back in place'. 'Out, you fool!' shouted the king, 'And yours?' he asked, pointing to the third old hag. The third old hag said, 'Your Majesty, I can go to the sky, and return, and tear a part of it, and stitch it back in place.'

'You are the wisest, and you are the one I need. Now look at this shoe carefully. I want you to find its pair or I will have you crushed in the oil crusher.'

'Yes, your Majesty. If I fail, have me crushed in the oil crusher. But for my expedition, I want a boat and necessary provision, and the washerman and the two old hags here to come with me.'

Having been provided with all that she needed, the old hag sailed the boat upstream. At long last she reached the palace of the princess of the jungle.

Her guess was right. She saw the princess sitting alone, for her prince had gone out for a hunt. Time was on the side of the old hag. She was at first spellbound by the beauty of the princess, but she collected her wits for she was the worst of them all, the cleverest of the old hags.

Then she rushed to embrace the poor princess, crying and wailing.

The princess was perplexed. The old hag said in tears, 'You do not remember me at all, and how can you? It is ages since you last saw me. I am your aunt. Your dear mother, my worthy sister died in grief for you and since her death, it has been my one mission to find you. I have found you today after years of search.'

The poor princess was moved by her tears and tenderness. She welcomed her sincerely and prepared an excellent meal for her.

In the evening when the prince returned from the hunt, she introduced him to the old hag. He too was pleased and showed her all the respect due to an aunt of his wife.

Next day, when the prince was asleep after his lunch, the hag suggested to the princess that they go out to have a look at her beautiful forest. The princess could have no hesitation, so together they went out, laughing and chatting like young girls. The old hag cunningly led the princess to the bank of a river where her companions lay in wait. But before the princess could see them, the old hag suddenly stopped as if an idea had suddenly struck her.

'You stay here my poor child,' she said glibly. 'The prince is fast asleep and the door is wide open. Let me go back and close it, lest a wild beast should enter it and endanger the life of the prince.' Then without waiting for an answer, she rushed back.

The prince was sleeping soundly when she arrived, and so, with his own sword, she cut him in two. Having done this she came back to the princess, who was waiting at the same spot.

Then cleverly she led the princess to a waiting boat. She was now trapped. The washerman, and the two other hags tied up the princess, and the boat set sail. The princess wept and wailed, but there was none to listen to her or help.

After a journey of many days, the hag returned home and produced the princess before the king. She was a dazzling beauty, and the king decided to marry her. But she was so beautiful that the king did not have the courage to force her will. He, therefore, put the proposal to her gently.

The princess was wise. She knew that she could not bluntly refuse her captor. She promised to give her answer after two years, during which period she would be able to think and decide. The king agreed to wait.

The princess was lodged in a separate palace, where everything was provided for her comfort. A year and a half went by. Now she was beginning to lose all hope of seeing her prince again. The king, on the other hand, was making preparations for his marriage to her.

Now it so happened, that after years of travelling, the three friends of the prince, who had parted from him in the jungle, happened to come to the city where the princess was living, and entered into the service of the king.

One day while they were in the court, a bonny little boy ran in, chasing his ball. The boy was an exceptionally beautiful child. The herder was the first to notice that he had a striking resemblance to their friend, the prince. He hinted as much to his friends, but the carpenter laughed at the idea. Upon this the herder said that he had the talent to tell someone's ancestry even seven generations before him, and that he was absolutely sure that this was the prince's son.

He found the boy's ball, and also gave him sweets in order to cultivate his friendship.

The child came for sweets again the next morning, and then he started coming every day and played with the herder.

One day the herder put a piece of paper in his pocket, on which he wrote the name of the child's father, his friend, the prince.

Next day, the child returned with a letter from the princess in which she had confirmed the fatherhood of the child and had told her whole story.

This was happy news for the three friends who held a meeting to discuss how they could rescue the princess.

Then they wrote another letter to the princess, saying that she should arrange to get a certain kind of wood. The princess found the wood and the carpenter set to work. In a few days a flying divan was ready. Now there was only one day left in the two year period after which the princess had to marry the king, who had completed the preparations for the wedding.

That night the three friends stole into the palace garden with the flying divan, and hid it in a corner. Through their friend, the little boy, they sent a message to the princess to meet them at midnight with her child.

At the appointed time, the princess came strolling into the garden, with three of her best maids.

The men hesitated in taking the three maids on the flight but the princess said that she had brought them with a purpose, which she would disclose later.

There was not much time for argument anyway and they decided to act before the royal guards got wind of the clandestine activity in the garden. They, therefore, sat on the divan. The carpenter took the controls in his hands and the divan rose with a little jerk. In a few moments, they were flying above the clouds.

The princess knew the course, and she advised them to fly over the river, upstream. Flying day and night, they reached the jungle mansion of the princess, now in ruins. They descended and with a jerk, the flying divan came to a halt on the ground.

They rushed into the mansion, but they found only the bones of the prince whereupon the princess began to wail. The scholar advised her to be patient. Then he arranged the bones of the prince in the form of the living body. He covered this arrangement with a sheet of white cloth. Everybody watched him with great excitement.

The scholar then started muttering some prayers, and in a few moments, the prince came to life and sat up, full of health and radiance.

The princess embraced him and told him the whole story. The prince was overwhelmed with happiness.

Then the princess gave her three pretty maids in marriage to the three friends of her husband, and all the four couples lived happily ever after. Their seed grew, and in a few years a city sprang up where there was love and cooperation, and no ill will.

They say that this city still flourishes on the bank of a river in the Punjab. But the rivers change course and nobody can identify the river, because there are five rivers in the Punjab on whose banks many, many happy cities continue to flourish, fade away, and flourish again, while the wheel of time turns endlessly.

* * * * *

The Golden-Haired Princess

Long ago, there lived in a city a merchant who was known all over the world for his honourable dealings. He was charitable and generous, and was therefore highly respected. To this merchant was born a son, but as fate would have it, soon after the birth of the child, the father died.

The son was given a fair education, and was brought up in luxury by his able mother. When he came of age, his mother told him that his father was a merchant of great talent and he should, therefore, follow in the footsteps of his father.

But she did not want him to go to far off lands, because bread could be earned close to home. The boy did not agree, because he wanted a life rich with adventure. Besides, no young man likes advice. He argued with his mother until she agreed to grant him permission to travel as much as he wanted, for she loved him very much, and love makes one weak. She gave him three hundred rupees, and saw him off, her heart heavy with foreboding.

He went west, travelling through deserts and fertile plains, without a particular destination in mind. In a jungle he met a snake charmer who had a basket full of cobras. The boy wanted to buy one. The snake charmer was willing, and the bargain was struck at one hundred rupees.

After a few moons, he met a man who was selling parrots and was tempted to buy one. The price of one hundred rupees for a parrot was agreed upon and the boy got his bird.

Further on, he met a man selling cats. Again the boy was tempted, so after settling the price at one hundred rupees for a cat, he bought one. His three hundred rupees were thus spent, for which he had a cobra, a parrot, and a cat to carry. He decided to return home with this queer merchandise.

His mother kissed his forehead fondly when she saw him, then looked at his baggage. She could not understand. What would he do with a snake, a parrot, and a cat, she wondered. But she welcomed him anyway, saying nothing about his purchases.

The boy had no explanation for his queer acquisitions either. He sat quietly in a corner thinking. The cobra was watching him with its shining eyes. He suddenly spoke like a human being. He said, 'Do not worry my friend. I will fetch you more than the price you paid for me.' The parrot did not lag behind. He said, 'Do not worry about me either. Your money is safe.'

The cat cut in, 'And, indeed, you will not stand to lose for having bought me.'

The young man was encouraged. He started looking after his pets with great affection and hope.

One day the snake came into his bed when dawn was breaking. Whistling close to his ear, he woke him up. Then he told the young merchant that that was the day when he would be paid back for his friendliness and affection. He was no ordinary cobra; he was the only son of the king of cobras who lived in a certain jungle. The cobra wanted the young man to take him there. 'On our way to the place where my father lives there are lots of snakes and scorpions, but since I'll be with you they will do you no harm' the cobra told him, and went on, 'You must continue to advance towards the rose garden. My father the King Cobra will be sitting on his golden throne in the centre of the garden. You must proceed respectfully and deliver me to my father. The king will be overjoyed to see me, his son, and will want to reward you, but you must say, "No thanks. God has given me enough." The king will again ask you what you want, but you must make the same answer again. The king will feel somewhat challenged at that, and will ask you for the third time. That would be the right time for you to make your desire known. But before you speak, you should ask the king to give you his word of honour that he will grant you whatever you ask for. The king will hasten to give you his word of honour. You should then demand the pearl shining in his crown. That pearl has the power to grant any and all wishes of its owner.'

With the cobra curled round his neck, the young man left home for the jungle. It was a clear morning and the cobra showed him the way.

After many moons, and travelling through valleys and plains the two reached the kingdom of the King of Cobras.

There were all kinds of snakes and scorpions on the way, but no harm came to the young man.

As he reached the rose garden the snake guards made way for them, their noisy hissing sounding like the blowing of many bugles. The sound attracted the attention of the king who was enjoying his midday nap. As he approached the king, the young man uncurled the cobra from his neck, and placed it on the throne near its father. The king was overjoyed and offered to reward the young man.

But the young man, acting on the advice of his friend, said that he wanted nothing since God had given him everything. He repeated the same words when the king wanted to know his wish for the second time. He was asked to make his wish known for the third time. The young man now got the king to give him his word of honour, as planned, and then made his wish known. He asked for the pearl in the king's crown. The king, of course, was left with no choice but to part with his magic pearl.

In a moment the pearl was shining on the young man's palm. The young man looked at it with delight and said, 'O Pearl, I want to reach home at once.' It was no sooner said than done. He was already in his room, the pearl still on his palm.

Then he said, 'O Pearl, I want to have a house made of gold.' And it was no sooner said than done. He was already in a palace made of gold.

Then he said, 'O Pearl, I want to be a king.' And it was no sooner said than done. He was already sitting on a throne with a crown on his head, attended by a court full of courtiers.

Then he said, 'O Pearl, I want to marry a princess with golden hair.' And it was no sooner said than done. He was already sitting with his queen, the fairest woman of the world, with a head full of golden hair. They started living happily together.

One day this golden-haired queen went to a river, and took a bath. To dry her wet hair she sat down on the riverbank, and began to comb it. A few golden hairs stuck in the comb, so when she finished combing she washed the comb in the river and went home.

This bunch of golden hair floated down the river. Many kingdoms away, a prince caught sight of the golden hair, and was so fascinated that he decided to look for and marry the unknown woman with the golden hair.

He sent for the most cunning old woman in his kingdom, and told her that she must go in search of the girl with the golden hair and bring her to him, no matter how. The crafty woman accepted the assignment, and set out in a boat, upstream, to look for the girl with golden hair.

She made her boatmen row and row until they were dead tired. They rowed until winter was left behind and tiny flowers of spring began to dance in the wilderness of the jungle. Finally they reached the city where the golden-haired queen lived, a fact known to everybody.

She left her boat anchored, and went alone to the queen's palace. She was a master in the art of bluff, and she shouted at the guards for not making way for the queen's aunt, as soon as she reached the gate of the palace. Taken in by her assurance, the guards trembled with fear and made way, at the same time blowing their noisy trumpet in order to inform the queen of the royal guest's arrival.

The queen heard the trumpet and ran out of her chambers to welcome her guest whom she did not know at all. But the crafty woman was full of confidence. She advanced and embraced her 'niece', the golden-haired queen. The crafty woman told the queen that she did not know her at all because while she was only a child she, her aunt, had left for Makkah to pray at the House of God. She had now returned after many years spent in prayer, and as she was near the end of her days, she wanted to see her niece.

This was a moving story, well told. The queen was impressed.

She took her 'aunt' in, and made arrangements for her to stay in the chamber next to her own.

The old crook pretended to be all love and tenderness for her. Soon she learnt all the secrets of the palace.

She noticed that the king wore a ring, made of very ordinary metal, with a pearl set in it. But the prince never removed it from his finger, not even in the bathroom. This pearl intrigued the crafty mind.

One day, making her tongue sweeter than honey, she said to the queen, 'Why does the king wear that inferior metal? It is beneath his royal status.'

The princess smiled, and then answered that it was only apparently an inferior metal; and that they owed everything they had to the pearl that was set in it. And then she told the woman the whole story of the pearl which came from the King Cobra's crown.

The old crook seemed very pleased with this unusual story.

'But men are faithless,' she said cunningly. 'And you never know when they fall for another woman. You should, therefore, keep this ring in your own custody, unless you want to be one day thrown out in the street. In fact, my old eyes have seen so much in this world, that nothing can now cheat me. I have been suspecting the king. I feel that he is in love with some other princess already.'

'Impossible,' said the queen. But the more she thought of it the less she was sure. Women are quick to accept a suggestion like that.

The crook laughed at the innocence of the queen. Then she said, 'Well, try it tonight. Ask for the ring, and mark my words, he will never give it to you.'

This hit the mark. The queen was determined to test her husband's love for her.

When the king came home that night, the first thing the queen did was to demand the custody of the ring. At first the king tried to tell her that it was safer on his finger, but finding the queen adamant, he removed it from his finger, and put it on hers.

The queen was so pleased with her success that when the king went to sleep, she slipped into her 'aunt's' chamber to show her the ring.

The crook was full of approval. Then she suggested that the king should not have gone to sleep so soon, as it was a wonderful moonlit night, and on the bank of the river was a tribe of gypsies, performing deeds of magic, which the queen could have seen.

The queen was excited. She was ready to go to the river to see the gypsies and their tricks. The two women soon dressed, and from the back door of the palace, they sped to the riverbank, without anybody's knowledge.

Strolling along the river, the crook led the queen to her boat in which her men lay hidden. They pounced upon her, and gagging her mouth, put her in the boat, which soon set sail. The old hag untied her gag only after she had removed the ring from her finger, and then, in the twinkling of an eye, because of the ring, they were in the audience chamber of the other king, who was surrounded by all his courtiers.

The king called his son whose marriage was at once solemnized with the queen with the golden hair. The ring was also given to him, with the warning that if he lost it, he would lose the princess too.

Going back to our prince, the hero of this story, when he woke up in the morning he found himself in a jungle. Everything was gone with the ring. His parrot and cat sat silently under a tree.

The prince was dejected and silent, not knowing what to do. Seeing him thus, the parrot and cat decided to prove their worth. Without warning the prince, they slipped away, in search of their queen.

The cat walked by the river while the parrot flew overhead. When night came they rested together. After many moons, they reached the city where their queen was spending her days in a prison, for she had not accepted her new husband. They stole into her cell. She was overjoyed at seeing her friends, and saw a ray of hope in their arrival.

The parrot asked her about the whereabouts of the ring. She told them that it was with the prince. During the day he wore it on his finger and at night when he went to sleep, he kept it in his mouth so that nobody would steal it.

The cat thought that it was easy to steal it and she would manage it. The parrot was willing to cooperate. When night fell and the prince went to sleep, the cat and the parrot entered his chambers. The cat went into his bed, and with the soft hairs of its tail tickled the rim of the sleeping prince's nose. The prince sneezed and the ring fell out of his mouth. The parrot pounced on it and picking it up with his crooked beak flew away with it.

The cat walked by the river while the parrot flew overhead. In a few days they were back with their prince, who was sitting all alone in the jungle where he had lost everything. He was extremely pleased to get the pearl back.

Holding the pearl again in his hand, he said, 'O pearl, I want my golden palaces back'. And it was no sooner said than done.

Then he said, 'O Pearl, I want my kingdom restored.'

And it was no sooner said than done.

Then he said, 'O Pearl, I want my queen of the golden hair back.'

And it was no sooner said than done. The princess stood before him, sparkling with beauty like dew on rose petals. The king embraced her tenderly.

Seeing the two united, and having done their duty, the cat and parrot, much against the wishes of their master, left to follow their own interests.

They went away and nobody ever saw them again. But people continue to keep cats and parrots in the hope that they will prove to be as good friends to them as they were to the prince.

It is also stated that the king died very old, but when he died, the pearl went back to the king of cobras. Snake charmers continue to charm snakes in the hope that they will charm the son of the King Cobra, someday, and take him back to his father for a reward. They remember that it is the third time, and only after they have the king's word of honour, that they should make their wish for the pearl known, when they have the king's son curled round their neck. But many, alas, have lost their lives to the venom of the snakes in this foolish pursuit; and many more may still do so.

* * * * *

Fate Versus Wisdom

The youngest of the seven sons of a Hindu shopkeeper was the only one with some sense. The other six were plain fools. When the wise son grew up, he went to his father and sought his permission to do some business independently.

His father was a poor shopkeeper, with no capital to spare. How could he help?

The wise son said that travelling was a blessed activity. He should, therefore, be allowed to go to some other city and try his luck. To this the shopkeeper agreed and his son departed for lands unknown.

Now Fate and Wisdom were watching the situation with great interest. Fate said that it would put the boy in impossible situations, for upsetting the peace of the home. Wisdom accepted the challenge and said it would help the boy out of all entanglements of fate. The wise boy continued his journey while this happened, quite ignorant of what was brewing.

He arrived in another city, sought out the king's palace and standing near its rampart shouted at the top of his voice, 'Have wisdom, but no money! Have wisdom, but no money.'

The king heard these strange words, and sent his royal guards to fetch the man who was uttering them.

In a moment the boy stood before the king, but he neither trembled with fear, nor laughed like a fool. Solemn and serene he stood, ready to answer any question.

The king looked at him and said, 'What were you saying outside my palace?'

The boy respectfully answered, 'I was saying, Your Majesty, that I had wisdom but no money.'

'What would you do with the money if you got some?' enquired the king.

'I would invest it in business and would return it after earning some profit,' said the boy.

The king was impressed with the boy's self confidence. He ordered that ten thousand rupees be immediately given to the boy. This was done.

The boy counted the money and then submitted that the money be given to him as a gift and not as a loan.

But why? Asked the king. 'You said you wanted to return it.'

'Yes, Your Majesty,' answered the boy, 'But I might run into losses, or maybe, I become dishonest after I have the money in my hand. In that case, I would be immoral, which I would never want to be.'

The king gifted the money. The boy took leave of the king, and taking with him two servants, left the city.

Fate and Wisdom started an argument. Wisdom, said, 'I got him ten thousand rupees from the king under your nose. Do you accept defeat?'

Fate smiled, 'But you should wait and see the end. I will not let him succeed.'

They followed the young man who reached a city he had never seen before. His shoe was broken during the long walk, so he went to a cobbler as soon as he arrived in the city.

The cobbler was sharpening his knife on a stone. The boy soon noticed that it was a priceless stone, perhaps a large diamond, with a ruby in it, and the cobbler knew nothing about it. The boy bought this stone for a mere coin, which the cobbler thought was excessive. Both parties parted happily, believing themselves richer than before.

The wise boy returned to the king, his benefactor, and showed him the stone, which he said he had bought for ten thousand rupees. The king, however, could not see the treasure in this dirty piece of stone. He was rather amused and threw it in a corner of his palace.

The boy requested that he be granted ten thousand rupees once more so that he could go on a trading mission again. Amused as the king was, he gave him the money.

The boy left the city with his two servants and went in a different direction this time. When they came upon a river, he decided to camp on its bank.

They built a small hut, and from a village close by they bought a buffalo so they could have its milk.

The boy dug the ground and made a receptacle there, in which he poured the buffalo milk that was in excess of their needs, until the receptacle was full to the brim.

Now, a pair of white ducks which were flying overhead in search of food thought of having a drink. They descended and had their fill of the sweet buffalo milk.

The duck felt very obliged, and when they had finished, she said to her drake, 'We have drunk the poor fellow's milk without permission. We must pay for it.'

The drake agreed, and together they went to the river. They dived into it and came out with a matchless pearl each in their beaks. This they threw in the receptacle of milk.

It then became their daily practice. Each day they came in the morning, drank milk in return for two matchless pearls, and flew away.

The wise boy was observing all that happened. As soon as the ducks flew off after casting pearls in the milk can, he would pick up the pearls and hide them in dung cakes, normally used for making a fire. In a few days he had a heap of dung cakes drying in the sun, with a matchless pearl in each of them without anybody getting to know of it.

After many days, a peasant happened to pass that way. He did not expect to see a house in this wilderness. He was hungry and tired, and so he came running to the hut. Close to the hut he found a shoe which was dirty and dusty. He picked it up.

He was warmly welcomed and given food and bed. In the morning when he was leaving, he thought of paying for the hospitality he had received, but he had nothing except the dusty old shoe. He offered it with great humility.

The boy washed the shoe clean of dust and found that it was made of gold and rubies.

After a few more days, a group of traders who had lost their way, came to the hut for help. They had enough provisions but nothing to make a fire with. They happened to be traders from the kingdom whose king had gifted ten thousand rupees twice to the boy, and they recognised him.

They needed the dung cakes, which they could see in heaps in front of the hut, and were willing to pay any price for them.

The boy was equally willing to give them as many dung cakes as they wanted, on the condition that they would return the same kind of dung cakes when both parties went back to the kingdom. The traders willingly agreed, and took more than they actually needed. But the dung cakes that were given to them by the wise boy, were not the ones with pearls. They were ordinary.

The traders made fire, spent the night and left for home. After a few days, the wise boy followed them, with all the dung cakes loaded on a bullock cart, the ones with pearls hidden among them.

Wisdom said to Fate, 'Now you watch again. The young man is a success.'

In the absence of the wise boy, a great jeweller had been the guest of the king. The cobblers' stone, which had been lying in a corner of the palace since the king threw it there, caught his eye. He picked it up and went to the king, saying, 'This is a marvel, Your Majesty, a priceless stone with a ruby, and it lies unnoticed!'

The king wondered at this discovery. He had the stone washed, and sent it to the treasury. For the first time he gave the boy credit for some wisdom. But where was the boy?

The boy reached the capital of the king one day after the traders, who had appeared before him with tales of their travels, and the gifts they had brought.

The boy went to the court with two dung cakes and caught hold of the traders, saying to His Majesty that they were his debtors.

The leader among them stated in the presence of the king that they were indeed his debtors, but they owed him only some dung cakes, which they were willing to return.

The boy affirmed their statement and taking out the dung cakes he had with him, broke them into two. Sparkling pearls fell out of them dazzling everybody's eyes. Picking them up, the boy said, 'They owe me dung cakes each containing pearls like the ones I gave them, like the ones I have shown here to Your Majesty.'

The traders turned pale. Not all their wealth could buy them enough pearls. They begged the king for mercy.

The boy told the whole story to the king, who was very pleased with the wisdom of the boy.

'Wisdom said to Fate, 'Look at the boy's success. He has won again!' But Fate smiled, and said, 'Wait and see the end. I can yet turn the tables.'

The boy presented the golden shoe to the king as a gift. The king was pleased. He sent it to his dearest queen.

When the king went to his chambers at night he found his beloved queen dejected, and lying on an old and broken cot, a sure sign of great distress.

The king was worried and asked the queen what was wrong. The queen told him with tears streaming down her delicate cheeks, that she must have the other shoe in the pair, or else she would kill herself.

The king immediately called the wise young man and ordered him to produce the other shoe.

The boy was troubled at this impossible demand, but finding no way out, asked for a month's time, and left the city early in the morning. He took with him a bottle of liquor.

Soon he reached his old hut, and putting it in order with the help of his two servants, started living in it.

It so happened that the peasant who had given him the shoe had again lost his way in his useless travels, and was again hungry and tired. He was glad to see the hut come to life, and walked towards it. Precisely at the same spot as he had found one shoe from a pair, he found the other shoe, covered with dirt and dust. He picked it up. At the hut he was welcomed as before, and given a good dinner. The peasant gave his host the other shoe, and started talking.

The wise boy thought that the daughter of the king was now of age, and was a pampered girl. If she suddenly decided to marry the owner of the golden shoes, it would be terrible. How would he then find the owner of the shoe?

The peasant was in a joyful mood, and chatting away. The boy brought out his bottle of liquor, and made him drink the whole of it. The peasant was soon knocked out, and fast asleep.

The boy tied him to his horse's back, and riding fast, reached the city before dawn. He went straight to the king with the shoe.

The king was very pleased with the wise young man. He sent the second shoe to the queen, who now beamed like the sun.

Wisdom said to Fate, 'Do you see the success of the boy?' 'Yes,' said Fate. 'But wait and see the end. I will yet ruin him.'

At night when the king was in the queen's chambers, she said, 'Our daughter has now grown up. We must find a match for her.'

'Yes, I think we should,' replied the king.

'I would like to marry our daughter to the prince who owned the golden shoes. If he wears shoes of such beauty, how beautiful he himself must be!'

The king liked the suggestion. In the morning he called the wise young man and ordered him to produce the prince of the golden shoes, or he would be buried alive.

The young man was expecting this assignment. He took a month's leave, and left the city, taking the peasant with him. He went to a far off city, and took suitable lodgings there. Here he had the peasant dress well, eat well, and taught him princely manners. His hair was cut like a prince and his whiskers were shaved off. In a month, the peasant looked like a prince.

After a month, and with plenty of grooming, he presented the peasant who had learnt his lessons well, to the king, as the prince of the golden shoes.

The king approved of the elegant young man and betrothed his daughter to him. Preparations for a wedding feast were begun.

On the appointed day, the marriage took place, and the peasant became the husband of the princess.

The wise boy was not so sure of the manners and demeanour of the peasant. He was afraid.

Wisdom said to Fate, 'Look, I have made a prince out of a peasant.' Fate smiled, and said, 'But you wait and see the end. I can yet ruin him.'

The peasant went to the chambers of his princess wife, but he was afraid. He was not sure of himself.

He saw his wife. She was a dazzling beauty, the like of whom the poor peasant had never seen in his life. He could not bear it, and fainted.

The princess was a good wife, and so she was worried. She put him in bed, and placing his head on her lap, started fanning him with the corner of her royal robe. She was nervous. She could not understand it. She thought that her husband was perhaps too great a king to accept her as a wife. He had perhaps not liked her.

Soon the peasant came to. She asked him meekly, 'Do you not like me, Sir?'

The peasant could not answer this simple question. He was all the more nervous, and in confusion he said, 'Please open these windows.'

The princess opened the windows, whereupon the peasant jumped out of one of them.

The royal guards thought that this was a thief, trying to escape. They pounced upon him, caught him, and took him to their officer.

The king having been informed that a thief had been caught jumping out of the princess' chambers, ordered him to be beheaded. The peasant was taken to the slaughter pad immediately.

Now Fate spoke. She said to Wisdom, 'You had a peasant made king. But I am going to have him killed. Let us see if you can still save him,' Wisdom smiled, and said, 'Wait and see the end. He is not dead yet.'

The news soon spread in the city. The wise boy understood the whole situation. He rushed to the slaughter pad, and warned the royal guards that they were killing no thief, but the king's own son-in-law.

The royal guards started trembling with fear. They rushed to the king and told him the whole story. The king came out in person, and brought the peasant back to the chambers of his daughter with a thousand apologies. Fate had lost the game.

Wisdom said, 'I have defeated you. The peasant is now a king.'

Fate accepted defeat. That night was a very pleasant and long one for the peasant prince.

In the morning, when the princess and the peasant prince were taking a bath, the wise son of the Hindu shopkeeper was taking leave of the king, his train of mules loaded with gold and silver, and his great horse neighing in anticipation of the journey.

He was the wise young man who defeated Fate.

* * * * *

The Cat Princess

In olden times, there lived a king, who had seven wives. Wealthy as he was and happily married too, he was dejected because he was without an issue.

One day he called his seven queens, together, and declared that if they remained barren, he would have them killed.

The queens started trembling with fear. They looked at each other in helplessness. Then the youngest of them all, who was also the wisest, requested that they be granted a year, at the end of which, if they failed to bear him a child, they could be put to death.

Finding this reasonable, the king agreed.

The seven queens went to their chambers and started praying. Days turned into nights while they prayed, But they remained barren.

On the last day of the year, they had a long meeting, after which they decided that they should announce the pregnancy of the youngest queen, and maybe Allah would show mercy and turn falsehood into truth later, if they lived.

The king was very pleased with this announcement, and everybody's life was spared. He even celebrated the occasion and opened the gates of his treasure houses for the needy.

Eight months passed, and the queens started to worry, but there seemed to be no way out. At the end of the ninth month, when she was expected to give birth to a child, the youngest, who was the wisest, thought of a plan. She let it be known that her labour pains had started.

Secretly she had arranged with the maids and nurses, astrologers and divines, to say to the king that a girl had been born, but that there were omens which indicated that the king should not see his daughter until she was fourteen or he would instantly die. At the same time, she adopted a newborn kitten, which screamed like a human child.

The king was left with no choice but to accept the dictates of fate, though it was terrible for him not to see his only offspring for such a long time. He started giving more time to the affairs of the state, to divert his attention.

Ten years passed by. The king was kept informed about the health and beauty of the princess, who in fact did not exist, and her fine education and understanding, which was only a tale. In the name of his daughter, he was also given advice by the queens, on how to conduct some of his affairs, because the princess was reputed to be wise.

The king loved his imaginary daughter. After her tenth year had supposedly passed, the queens suggested that the king should find a suitable match for her, so that she was not late for marriage when the time came. This reminded the king of a father's foremost duty, and he sent emissaries to the four corners of the earth, one of whom returned with a suitable proposal.

The proposal was accepted, and the marriage fixed. The appointed day brought the bridegroom with his royal party to the king's palace. While the king was busy with the marriage arrangements, the queens called the bridegroom in. The prince went in, unaccompanied, to his mother-in-laws' chambers. When they saw him, all the queens fell at his feet. He was puzzled, and shyly he asked them what the matter was.

Finding him sympathetic, they told him the whole story.

This was a noble young prince, kind of heart, and full of understanding. He could not bear to think that seven old ladies would lose their heads. He agreed to keep their secret.

The marriage was performed normally, and in accordance with custom, the prince's party departed with great dignity. The palanquin that followed his horse, contained the cat that was supposed to be his bride, eleven years of age.

Reaching home, the prince told his mother that no one could see his bride until she was fourteen, and hence, she would be lodged in a separate palace. The mother agreed.

The prince lodged the cat in the bridal chambers where he spent his nights like a loving husband, playing with the cat. The queen mother looked after the house in the day, cleaned and swept the room, as no one else could go inside. The cat remained hidden, while she worked.

The queen mother was old and weary, and had married her son off with fond hopes that her daughter-in-law would take charge of her affairs, keep house, and clean and sweep, but her hopes had vanished. One day she complained of her bad luck. The prince was worried. He did not want his mother to work, and he could not tell her the truth. On the other hand, she was forming an evil opinion of his wife. He told her that he wanted her to rest, and she should leave the house to her daughter-in-law. The mother agreed. The cat overheard this conversation, and she decided to take up her wifely duty of housekeeping.

Next morning the cat woke up early, and tied a piece of cloth to the end of her tail. With it she swept the rooms clean of dust, and arranged everything in place. The prince was more than pleased.

She was about to be fourteen now, and it would be time for her to go to her father for the first time. The prince's mother was also counting the days in the hope that she would see her daughter-in-law. But the seven queens were extremely worried. The prince too was dejected, anticipating that his marriage to a cat would not remain undiscovered and when it was revealed, it would make everybody laugh at him. He was also worried about the lives of the seven queens which he had tried to save, but which he would not be able to save when the truth was found out.

One day, while the cat was sweeping the floors with a piece of cloth tried to her tail, a demon and a fairy flew overhead, and saw this strange spectacle.

The fairy invited the attention of the demon to it, but he did not care, and urged her on.

The demon loved the fairy, and she was stubborn. She stopped and refused to go any further until she had learnt all about the strange sight she saw. The demon could not refuse her. He stopped too, and told her that the cat was actually a princess, who had been turned into her present form by a demon friend of his.

The fairy now insisted that she be brought back to her human form. The demon said that it was easy. She should anoint herself with the oil of the lamps that burnt at night in her chambers. The cat was listening to this conversation, and no sooner did the fairy and the demon leave, she went to her chambers, took all the oil from the lamps, and anointed her body with it. She saved one finger though, whereby she could prove to the prince her husband, that she was the same old cat. And in a moment there stood before the empty old lamps, a princess of matchless beauty, young and smiling, whose one finger resembled a cat's claw.

In the evening, when the prince came to his bedchamber, he was greeted by the beautiful princess. He was confused. He wanted to go back, whereupon the princess said, 'Why do you go back, sir? I am your wife.'

The prince did not know what to say. He mumbled, 'I was looking for my cat. Do you know where she is?'

The princess laughed and told him the whole story. The prince was overjoyed, and he spent a happy night with his wife for the first time.

In the morning, he took her to his mother who embraced her fondly and kissed her forehead, with many sweet wishes.

After a few days, he left with his wife for the kingdom of his father-in-law where the king awaited the sight of his daughter. When he heard of the arrival of the party, he went out of the city with his courtiers and noblemen, to welcome them. Precisely at this time, the seven queens were preparing to commit suicide. They climbed to the top of the palace from where they planned to fall to their death, for they knew that the king would kill them after torturing them, which would be a far more painful death.

The party was approaching the palace with great pomp and splendour. When it drew closer the prince could see the queens arrayed for the jump. He immediately guessed their motive and waved at them to wait until he arrived.

The youngest of all the seven queens, who was the wisest, and was not young any more, saw the prince first. She also saw a beautiful princess riding by his side. Perplexed, she asked her six sister queens to wait for a while. And they held back to learn the truth.

The prince went straight up the stairs of the palace and told them the whole story. They were overjoyed, because their lives had been saved, and also because they now had a jewel of a daughter.

* * * * *

A Bad Bargain

Once upon a time there was an old couple who lived in a small village, alone and uncared for. They were near the end of their days and had therefore abandoned all hope of a better life and worked just enough to fill their stomach.

The old man picked wood from the jungle and the old woman did their meagre cooking.

Close to their hut was a mango tree laden with fruit, which they could not climb. They waited for the wind to blow so that the mangoes would fall from the tree and they could get some to eat.

One day the old man was sick, which was a good excuse for not going out to work, so there was no wood to make fire, and the hearth was cold. The old woman tried to make the old man move out of his bed, but he pretended to be asleep. She knew that the old man loved sweet rice *pilau,** which he had not eaten for a long time. So, into his ear, she murmured 'If you go and get some wood today, I will cook sweet rice *pilau* for you.' The old man opened his eyes and taking his axe, left for the jungle, without a murmur.

He gathered the wood with great speed, and had started to make a bundle of it when suddenly he saw a bear approaching. He stood silent, trembling with fear.

This was a very kind and friendly bear who could see that the old man could not carry such a big bundle of wood, and he told him so.

The old man was encouraged by the bear's kindness. He said, 'It is true that this load is too much for my weak shoulders. But the old woman has promised me a dish of sweet rice pilau which I have not eaten for a long time. I will therefore have to try to carry the load.'

---

* *Pilau*: Oriental dish of rice with meat, spices, etc.

'Dish of sweet rice *pilau*, did you say? asked the bear, his mouth watering.

'Yes, indeed,' answered the old man. 'A whole dish of sweet rice *pilau* for me.' 'It must be a splendid dish!,' said the bear. He had often heard about it, but never tasted it, and this seemed to be his only chance.

'If I carry the wood for you, will the old woman give me some sweet rice *pilau*?' asked the bear like a hungry and innocent child.

The old man thought for a while, because he did not know if the old woman would part with a morsel or two. Then he answered, 'Yes, why not? But you do not know that sweet rice *pilau* is a very costly dish. If you carry two such loads on your back, then perhaps my old wife can afford to give you a nice helping. I will urge her to do so, because you are such a good bear.'

The old man patted the back of the bear on which he was to place two loads of wood.

The bear agreed to carry two loads of wood to the old couple's home. The old man took with him just enough wood for cooking the meal that day. He left the rest for the bear to bring later, and returned home.

Back at home, he told the whole story to the old woman, who immediately lighted a fire, and started to cook sweet rice *pilau*.

The bear was looking for ropes in the jungle which he could not find. He then tried to tie up wood with soft tree branches. It took a lot of time.

Meanwhile, the old woman cooked sweet rice *pilau* which was exceptionally delicious that day. They ate their fill, and leaving some for the bear in the pan, went inside the hut.

The old man had his stomach full, but greed lurked in his eyes. When the old woman went to fetch some water, he stole a part from the bear's share and ate it. He was wiping his mouth with his old shirt, when the old woman came back, pitcher on head and saw him stealing.

She did not say anything to the old man but she thought that she had a better right to steal from the bear's share. So she took some too.

The old man was watching from behind the door of the hut and now saw no reason not to eat a little more himself. He went ahead and started to eat out of the bear's share openly. The old woman came running and started eating too, and soon there was not a grain of rice left in the pot. They wiped it clean, laughed at the bear's foolishness and went back to their beds.

But the bear was now coming with his load of wood. He was panting and breathless. He threw the bundle of wood under the mango tree and started to call the old man.

The old people were not afraid. They slipped out of the rear window to avoid the bear.

The bear waited for some time, then started to look for the sweet rice *pilau*. He could still smell the wonderful aroma of the dish and nosing in the darkness, he came upon the pan but it was empty. He was disgusted and angry. He decided to punish the old couple.

He climbed on the mango tree and shaking it violently, let all the fruit fall, which he put into the pan and took away with him, leaving the old couple with no fruit and no pan to cook their food in.

He was not gone far when the old man, who was watching all this from behind his hut, suddenly sneezed. The bear was startled and he thought that somebody had fired a gun. Throwing away the fruit and the pan, he ran away as fast as his legs could carry him into the jungle. He was such a simpleton!

Old people are wise, and wise people sometimes exploit simpletons. The old couple returned and had a hearty laugh at the foolish bear, who got nothing for his labour.

* * * * *

The Foolish Crocodile

A fox used to drink water from a river in which there lived a crocodile. Whenever a foolish beast came there, the crocodile would pull him down by his leg, and make a good meal out of him.

The fox was cunning, which made him more attractive prey for the crocodile. He wanted very much to eat the fox's brains in order to learn some of his cunning. But the fox managed to keep away from the crocodile. Seeing this, the crocodile hid himself in shallow waters for many days. He did not catch any prey, and let word spread in the jungle through a crow, who often ate his leftovers, that he had migrated downstream.

Everybody but the fox believed the news and started to come to the river freely, drink water and bask in the sun. The fox was cautious as usual.

One day the fox came to drink at his usual spot. But the crocodile, in order to give the impression that he lay hidden there, had made the water muddy, while actually he was further down the stream. Deceived for once, the fox now went to drink downstream. By doing so he fell into the crocodile's trap who caught him by his leg.

The fox was clever and calm. He did not raise an alarm and did not try to extricate his leg from the jaws of the crocodile. Instead, he let it lie there lifelessly and shouted 'Mr Crocodile, please help me pull my foot out of the slime. It is stuck there. Good Mr Crocodile, please spit out that root in your mouth and help me. My leg is here.' And he shook his other leg.

The foolish crocodile thought that he was holding a root in his jaws while the leg of the fox lay in front of him. He released his leg whereupon the fox immediately jumped out of the water. Outside he had a hearty laugh at the crocodile.

The crocodile was insulted. He decided to try again.

The fox came again the next day, but he was now very careful. He wanted to be sure that he was not likely to be trapped again. He stood on the bank and said loudly to himself, 'The water here seems dangerous, because there are no bubbles today. The crocodile is certain to be hiding here.'

The crocodile was fooled and in order to show that he was not hiding there, started to blow bubbles to the surface of the water.

The fox went downstream, drank water, and coming back to the first spot said in a loud voice, 'Go on fasting my friend, because you will never catch me. I will not drink here today.'

Saying this he ran away. The crocodile waited, but the fox never returned, and his hunger became unbearable. Besides he had lost prestige in the eyes of other animals.

The fox found a spring where he could drink without fear. But he loved mangoes, which grew on the riverbank. He used to go there to eat mangoes and enjoy himself.

The crocodile knew this and thought of catching him under the mango trees.

He lashed the trees with his tail and brought down all the fruit. Then he made a big heap of mangoes, under which he hid himself.

The fox came as usual, and saw a big heap of mangoes, where he used to find only a few. He was suspicious. He stood at a distance and said to himself loudly, 'The mangoes used to roll down to me every day when I came. But today they are lying in a heap. There is something wrong.' The crocodile heard him, and in order to show that nothing was wrong, started to throw some mangoes towards the fox. The fox picked up the fruit, thanked the crocodile for his service and went away, laughing. He composed a beautiful verse in memory of his victory and sang it too,

Under the heap of mangoes
Lies hidden the enemy
Fools are beating their breasts
While the wise are eating fruit.

The crocodile was mad with anger. He decided to catch him or die.

The fox lived in a hole not far from the river. The crocodile slipped into it, sure that he would catch him in the evening.

The fox returned in the evening and saw footprints of the crocodile leading into the hole. He sang,

Home, O Home
Why do you not say welcome?

The foolish crocodile at once answered,
Long live, O my dear fox,
and welcome!

The fox laughed quietly and answered,
Home, sweet Home
Let me live for some time more!

The fox went and gathered dry branches of trees and bushes, which he stuffed in the hole and set ablaze. The crocodile was roasted alive.

It is said that since then, no fox drinks at the river for fear of revenge. It is also said that the brute in the water has still not learnt his lesson, as brutes seldom do.

* * * * *

The Timid Tiger

A tiger came upon a peasant who was ploughing his field. They saw each other. The tiger was pleased for he was hungry. The peasant had no gun, nor any help at hand. He started trembling with fear, and stood watching the tiger silently.

The tiger came close, and said, 'Well, I am not bad at heart and am willing to spare your life. But you will have to part with one of your oxen. I am hungry.'

The peasant could not refuse to part with an ox, for in that case the tiger would eat him. On the other hand if he allowed the tiger to feast on one ox, he would never have a pair of oxen again, and how would he plough his land then? He did not know what to do. He thought for a while, then an idea suddenly came to him, and he said, 'O king of the jungle, I have a suggestion worthy of your consideration...'

'Speak at once,' roared the tiger impatiently.

'You are hungry, my lord,' said the peasant. 'All you want is something to eat. If I give you my ox, I will not be able to plough my land with one ox, and my children will starve to death, which you do not want'.

'I do not want that,' confirmed the tiger. 'It is true.'

'Then, what if I bring you my cow? It is a fat animal,' suggested the peasant. 'Fat and tender, easy to tear into.'

'Well, make haste then,' said the tiger. 'I won't wait long.'

'I won't be long, sir,' said the peasant and ran towards his home.

His wife was a wise and brave woman, and when she heard his story, she advised him not to worry, as she would settle the matter.

The peasant was not sure. But his wife advised him to return to the tiger and to say that the cow had gone out grazing, and his wife was therefore bringing their horse for the tiger's meal.

Now, as luck would have it, this tiger was very fond of horse meat, and he rather welcomed this offer.

While the tiger awaited the horse meat, the peasant's wife let loose her long hair, put black paint on her face, and with streaks of red flowing down from her mouth, and a scythe in her hand, she followed her husband on horseback to the spot where the tiger stood waiting for his meal. She looked like a she-demon.

Fearlessly she advanced towards the two and taking a good look at the tiger she said to her husband 'What shall I do with just this, one, lean tiger? Where are the other three? I want to eat all the four together.'

The tiger was scared. He was scared because this strange she-demon had said that she could not do with less than four tigers for a single meal. But he stood there, watching.

The peasant's wife got off the horse, and scythe in hand, advanced towards the tiger saying, 'Well, I suppose I can at least make a beginning on this one.'

Hearing this, the tiger ran as fast as his legs would carry him. Meanwhile, a wolf was standing behind a bush watching the whole episode. He was surprised to see the king of the jungle taking to his heels in such desperation. He guessed that the peasant's wife had made a fool out of him, so he went running after the tiger.

The wolf told him that he had been fooled by a simple peasant woman and that if he had not stood his ground before, he should return and face the woman now. The tiger would not believe him, but so sure did the wolf seem of what he said that the tiger agreed, though on the condition that the wolf would go with him. He insisted that the wolf tie his tail to his, so that he could not run away leaving him alone if it was found that the she-demon was indeed real. The wolf made no objection to this.

When the two beasts got there, the peasant and his wife were still in their field, laughing at the incident. Then they saw the tiger and the wolf. The peasant became nervous, but his wife sat calmly watching the animals draw nearer.

When the two came close, she said furiously to the wolf, 'You promised to bring four tigers for my meal, whereas you are dragging just one lean beast with your tail. What shall I do with this monkey?'

The tiger froze with fear. The peasant woman came forward saying, 'Well, I can make a beginning with this one, though....'

Hearing this, the tiger took one great leap in the direction of the jungle, and ran for his life dragging the wolf behind him. The poor wolf bled profusely as he was dragged over sharp rocks, thorny bushes and fallen branches, and he soon died. Meanwhile, the peasant and his woman had a hearty laugh at the timidity of the tiger and the uncalled for interference of the wolf in matters which did not concern him.

* * * * *